ROLL THE WAGONS

William Heuman

CENTER POINT LARGE PRINT
THORNDIKE, MAINE

This Center Point Large Print edition
is published in the year 2022 by arrangement with
Golden West Inc.

Copyright © 1951 by Fawcett Publications, Inc.

All rights reserved.

Originally published in the US by Gold Medal Books.

The text of this Large Print edition is unabridged.
In other aspects, this book may vary
from the original edition.
Printed in the United States of America
on permanent paper sourced using
environmentally responsible foresting methods.
Set in 16-point Times New Roman type.

ISBN 978-1-63808-562-1 (hardcover)
ISBN 978-1-63808-566-9 (paperback)

The Library of Congress has cataloged this record
under Library of Congress Control Number: 2022944072

Chapter One

At two o'clock in the afternoon the sky took on a brassy look. This was the evil hour for freighting men on the trail, and Kern Harlan, wagonmaster for Rocky Mountain Freighting, remembered that he'd seen more fights between the men at this hour than at any other hour during the day or night. He had the feeling that something was brewing now between the bullwhackers on his Number Four and Number Five wagons.

It was in the way they walked beside their wagons, big shoulders hunched, staring straight ahead of them, jaws set, dirty flannel shirts drenched with perspiration; it was in the way they plodded through the six-inch dust of the trail, cracking their blacksnake whips occasionally, but not saying anything. That was always a sign. When a bullwhacker didn't swear at his animals, swear at the weather, at the dust, at the eternal chirping of the crickets, at everything in general, it mean that trouble was in the offing.

Riding his buckskin horse at the head of the column of thirty big Studebaker wagons, Kern glanced back. He felt the heat himself now, and he was up on a horse while the teamsters walked beside their plodding oxen. There were no clouds in the sky, and the sky stretched from the north to the south and from the east to the west as far as the eye could see, with only low, rolling hills to break the monotony of it. It was a treeless plain, the Denver Trail cutting straight across it, stretching into the distance, a ribbon of plowed-up dirt, pounded by the hoofs of a thousand teams of oxen that had gone over it this season alone, worn a foot deep into the prairie soil.

Before the big freighting wagons had struck out west from Nebraska City on the Missouri to Denver and to other points west, the covered wagons of the emigrants had rolled across these open plains, following the faint trails of the Indians and the mountain men who had gone before them. Wheels and hoofs and the hard heels of cursing, sweating bullwhackers had made this trail, and over it someday would roar the iron horses of the railroad.

Everett Green, commissary for this outfit, rode up on a sorrel horse, shaking his head as he drew abreast of Kern. Green was a spare, dour man, long in the employ of Rocky Mountain Freighting Company. He spat and said with a nod of his head toward the rear, "It'll be a fight when we reach Rock Springs this afternoon."

Kern nodded. "Number Four and Number Five," he mused. "I saw it."

"O'Keefe and Bannister," Green told him. "Two good men."

"What brought it on?" Kern asked. He listened to the creak and rumble of the big wagons behind him, and he watched the heat devils up ahead. Heading east toward Nebraska City, still two days from the home port, he felt the sun on his right side, searing him.

"What brought it on?" Everett Green repeated, and he looked up at the blue sky, at the distant hills, at the ears of his sorrel horse. "What brings any of it on, Kern?" he mused. "Maybe the heat; maybe being away too long from women; maybe just seeing each other every day for a month at a stretch, and getting tired of the same faces around you. You walk behind a man every day for a month, and after a while you just get tired of looking at his back; you begin to curse that back and the man who owns it. Maybe that's the way it is with O'Keefe and Bannister."

Kern smiled. "They'll have it out tonight," he said, "and they'll feel better in the morning."

Green said, "Don't figure they'll wait till camp tonight. It's now they're sore."

"Two o'clock in the afternoon," Kern murmured.

"In the morning they're fresh," Green said. "After the midday stop they have their bellies full. Late in the afternoon they know they'll be stopping pretty soon. At two o'clock there's just nothing—just the heat and the rumble of the wagons, and the stupid oxen beside them, and the man up ahead."

Kern looked back again—thirty wagons moving up over the brow of a low hill, thirty wagons with the big tarpaulins drawn across the tops and a few of the night herdsmen sleeping on top of them, sleeping in the glare of the sun. Thirty men strode beside the thirty wagons, each with his blacksnake whip in his hand, each with his own thoughts, the dust of the wagon ahead of him sifting back into his face, and twenty-seven long days of this behind him, no stopping points in between, no towns, no women, passing an occasional outfit headed the other way. Kern Harlan was glad that Nebraska City was only two days distant.

Behind the wagons came the small herd of spare oxen, kicking up a cloud of dust as they plodded along, the herders riding behind them, handkerchiefs drawn up across their faces.

Everett Green said, "We'll hit Rock Springs at about five o'clock. You'll be riding on, Kern?"

Kern nodded. "I'll be in Nebraska City before dark," he said. "Plenty to do." There was a shadow in his gray eyes now.

Green moistened his cracked lips and then wiped them with the back of his sleeve. "Be different," he said, "with Uncle Billy gone."

Kern nodded. He was staring at a banner of dust far off to the east, the dust undoubtedly of another freighting outfit heading west. He figured this outfit would pass them at about four o'clock in the afternoon. He tried to concentrate upon the banner of dust, upon the condition of the trail ahead of them, upon anything but the lovable Uncle Billy McCloud, his guardian, and until three weeks ago owner of Rocky Mountain Freighting.

Pulling out of Denver he'd received the news from a messenger sent out from the office that Uncle Billy had passed away very suddenly. For days he'd been stunned, unable to accept the fact. He'd been raised by Uncle Billy. As a small boy he'd sat on Billy McCloud's knee in his office, looking out the window, watching Rocky Mountain Freighting outfits roll into the yard from distant points. As Billy McCloud's ward he was to inherit Rocky Mountain Freighting. For seven years he'd been chief wagonmaster for the company, taking out the most important cargos, breaking all records on the trail. He was breaking the record from Denver to Nebraska City again this trip, breaking it by many days, but it didn't mean anything without Uncle Billy in the office to greet him when he came in, to smile at him, and to let him know that he was proud.

Everett Green squinted at the distant banner of dust. He said meditatively, "Reckon that could be another Ajax outfit, Kern?"

Kern shook his head. "They've grown like a mushroom this summer," he stated.

"And some mushrooms," Green frowned, "are

poisonous. I didn't like the looks of those Ajax outfits."

Kern didn't say anything. The previous spring Ajax Overland Freighting Company had been a new outfit in Nebraska City. He'd seen their wagon sheds and blacksmith shop going up. New Murphy wagons had been rolling off the Missouri River steamers, moving into the Ajax yard.

During the summer they'd evidently grown tremendously. It seemed that every other outfit they passed on the road bore the name Ajax on the tarpaulin lashed across the load.

Green said, "They can tell us how the water is at Rock Springs. If it's too low we'd better hole up at Silver Creek."

Kern was nodding his head in agreement when they heard the sudden whoop behind them. Without turning his head, Everett Green said a trifle wearily, "Reckon that's it, Kern."

Kern pulled up the buckskin and turned in the saddle. The wagon column had stopped. O'Keefe and Bannister, teamsters for the Number Four and Five wagons, were facing each other at a distance of about thirty feet, both with their blacksnake bull whips in their hands. Other bullwhackers were running up. The oxen stood in the yokes, heavy heads lolling. Sleepy-eyed night herders were sitting up on top of the wagons, looking around stupidly.

Bannister, a short, squat man with a brown

beard, stood with his heavy legs braced. He had a pair of tremendous forearms and a barrel chest. The back of his dirty gray flannel shirt was stained with sweat. He stood there, the whip in his hands, watching O'Keefe.

O'Keefe of Number Five wagon was taller, sandy-haired, long-necked. He had huge scoops for hands, and those hands were wrapped around the thick butt of the bull whip.

Everett Green said as they rode back toward the wagons, "Reckon it'll be with whips, Kern."

"No whips," Kern said briefly. He didn't like whip fights; these men were too expert with the long, curling lashes. Most of them could flick a fly off the ear of an ox at fifteen paces. He'd seen men lose eyes in fights like this, and both O'Keefe and Bannister were good teamsters. Tomorrow night in Nebraska City they would be drinking together, having forgotten entirely that there had been a disagreement on the trail.

Now it was two o'clock in the afternoon and the sun was pressing them down to earth with ruthless force. There was no shade; there was no breeze; there were no trees; just the sun and the eternal hills surrounding them, and always another hill to walk over. It seemed as if the saloons, the women, the good cheer of Nebraska City were still a thousand miles away.

Bannister uncoiled his blacksnake, making the buckskin popper snap with the force of a rifle shot. He circled a little, getting away from his own wagon, giving himself room to swing the whip.

O'Keefe came away from his wagon, too, his cracked lips tight, battered black hat pulled low over his eyes. He spat once as he moved away, and then he hitched at his belt with his hands.

The other teamsters formed a respectful circle, making little noise after the first outburst of excitement at the prospect of a fight. Possibly it was the knowledge that this was not going to be with fists but with whips that quieted them down. They'd all seen what the whips could do.

Kern dismounted leisurely and pushed through the circle. The two fighters were beginning to circle each other warily, holding their whips tensely now.

Kern drawled, "We'll put the whips down now, boys."

The two fighters stopped moving and looked at him. He was standing inside the circle, smiling calmly.

Bannister said thickly, "We draw Rocky Mountain pay, Kern, but this ain't Rocky Mountain business."

"You're fighting on Rocky Mountain time," Kern reminded him. "I'll tell you how to fight. Drop those whips."

"Hell with you," Bannister murmured. He took a firmer grip on his blacksnake and looked across at O'Keefe.

O'Keefe said tersely, "Our fight, Kern. Keep out of it."

Kern started to walk forward, still smiling. "Any fight on the trail," he stated, "is my fight, boys. You want to hold this up until you get in town?" He saw Everett Green grin. The commissary knew, too, that when they got in town the fight would be forgotten.

"We ain't holdin' nothin' up," Bannister growled.

Kern turned toward him, knowing that he was the one with whom he had to contend. O'Keefe might be reasonable about it, but Bannister was past words, past argument. He had to get this out of him—now.

Still smiling, walking toward him, Kern said gently, "You're a good teamster, Joe Bannister. Hate to see you lose an eye, or both eyes."

"Ain't losin' no eyes," Bannister said.

"Then put that whip down," Kern told him.

Bannister shook his head. He backed up another step, and that was as far as he was going. Kern saw that in his brown eyes. A kind of wildness had come into them. Bannister respected his wagonmaster, having been on the trail dozens of times with him, but in this one instance the bullwhacker was rebelling against authority.

It was the heat and the monotony, and not Joe Bannister.

Kern stopped about three feet from the man. He had a Colt gun on his hip, and he could have drawn the gun and asserted his authority that way. The teamster had his rifle on the wagon, but he didn't have a gun on his person. With a gun drawn on him he would have to give in, but Kern was aware that that was not the proper method. A gun meant that one man was better armed than another, not that he was a better man. This latter fact always had to be proved—every trip, every day on the long trail.

Bannister said, "Lemme finish this, Kern, an' then we'll get on with the haul."

Kern didn't say anything. He unbuckled his gun belt and handed it to Everett Green, who had stepped up behind him.

Bannister grimaced, watching him. He said, "Got no argument with you, Kern."

"I have one with you," Kern told him. He was still smiling as he lunged forward suddenly, butting Joe Bannister full in the stomach with his head, knocking him back toward his own wagon.

The breath left the teamster's body in one big belch. He dropped the whip, mouth wide open, gasping for air. Kern kept driving him back toward the wagon, lashing out with both fists to the stomach.

Bannister went down directly beneath the

water barrel lashed to the side of the wagon. He lay on his back, legs kicking, squirming. Kern straightened up, stepped to the water cask, and pulled the bung out. A torrent of water gushed out, falling across the bullwhacker, drenching him. He sat up, gasping, the water streaming down his face, and all the other teamsters roared with laughter.

The tension was broken. Even O'Keefe was grinning, the bull whip loose in his hands now. Bannister sat under the torrent of water until the barrel was empty. He just sat there, letting the water drench him, and then he got up, rubbing his stomach. He looked at Kern sheepishly, and the light was gone from his eyes. He said, "Reckon you're wastin' a lot o' good water on a bad bullwhacker, Kern."

"No hard feelings, Joe," Kern said.

Bannister grinned. He was cooled off by the drenching. He said, "Hell, I'm a Rocky Mountain man."

Kern Harlan said slowly, "That's the best recommendation anyone can have on the trail, Joe. Now push those bulls."

The teamsters plodded back to their wagons, yelling to each other good-naturedly. The night herders went back to sleep on top of the loads, and the dull-eyed oxen heaved into the yokes as the blacksnake whips cracked all along the line. Heavy wheels screeched unmercifully as they moved up the next grade, the mess wagon leading, festooned as usual with dry wood the cook had picked up along the way to be used for the fire that night.

Kern rode up to the head of the column again with Everett Green, and the commissary said to him, "That outfit is closer, Kern."

There was nothing said about the fight. It was an everyday incident on the trail, something better forgotten than remembered. Behind them O'Keefe and Bannister, the two recalcitrant bullwhackers, were trudging along beside their wagons, and the tension had gone out of them. The two-o'clock madness was over.

Kern Harlan studied the dust banner in the sky. He said, "We'll have a look at them, Everett."

Chapter Two

It was another half hour before they could see the wagons and the toiling teams of oxen moving toward them below the dust cloud. From the heavy rumble of the wagons Kern could tell that they were carrying good loads. He counted twenty wagons in the outfit, not including the mess wagon.

A squat, black-bearded bullwhacker in a dirty red flannel shirt stared at them suspiciously as they came up. He spat in the dust as he trudged beside his wagon, cracking his blacksnake.

Kern said to him, "Who's the wagon boss here?"

The bullwhacker caressed the thick butt of the whip. "Back there," he growled.

Kern saw him coming up, a thin man in a black coat, astride a chestnut gelding.

Green said, "Pioneer wagons, but I don't recognize any Pioneer teamsters."

Kern nodded to the wagonmaster, a freckled, long-nosed man, a stranger. Raised in Nebraska City, Kern knew every wagonmaster for every outfit. This man was new to the town.

"Any trouble here, mister?" the redhead rasped.

Kern looked at him. This kind of hospitality was new on the plains, also. Usually when one bull outfit passed another there was much good-natured jibing, and a brief visit by the wagonmasters, passing on news of the trail, best river crossings, grass, and other matters.

"No trouble," Kern told him briefly. "What outfit is this?"

"Ajax Overland," the wagonmaster snapped, "an' why?"

Everett Green said, "Some of those wagons are Pioneer Freighting." He nodded to a wagon just moving by, a big Murphy vehicle. The word Pioneer was scrawled in black across the canvas covering.

"Used to be Pioneer," the redhead told him sourly. "Ajax now. We bought out Pioneer."

Kern felt Everett Green staring at him, and he knew what the commissary was thinking. This new Ajax outfit had bought out old Jed Havemyer, who'd been in the freighting business as long as Uncle Billy McCloud himself. No one had ever expected Jed Havemyer to sell out. He was supposed to die in the traces, just as Billy McCloud had.

"Ajax bought out Pioneer," Everett Green repeated slowly. "You mean Jed Havemyer sold out?"

"I mean Ajax owns Pioneer," the wagonmaster snapped. "You understand English, mister?"

"The kind you're speaking," Green told him thinly, "hasn't been used too much on this trail."

"How's the water at Rock Springs?" Kern asked.

The redhead looked at him, a cold grin sliding over his face. "When you git there, mister," he chuckled, "you'll find out. We ain't doin' any favors for rival outfits on the Denver Trail."

With that he swung the chestnut horse around and trotted to the head of the column.

Everett Green said dryly, "Times are changing, Kern. If a man had given an answer like that ten years ago, he'd have been tarred and feathered."

"Why would Jed Havemyer sell out?" Kern asked as they rode back to their own outfit.

"Two reasons why a man quits the freighting business," Green observed. "He's fed up with it, or there's no business. We both know Jed Havemyer wouldn't get fed up with freighting. It's in his blood."

"There was plenty of business when we left," Kern murmured. "Still plenty of business as far as I can see."

"For Ajax Overland," Everett Green pointed out. "Maybe not for anybody else, the way it looks on this trail."

Kern didn't say anything, but he was frowning as they rode back to their wagons. In his years on the trail there had always been a half-dozen or more companies operating, and plenty of business for all. The Army was constantly putting up new outposts along the frontier, and thousands of tons of supplies and equipment had to be hauled into the interior. The Colorado gold fields in recent years had tremendously increased the demand for fast freighting, and there had always been business, contracts to be had for the asking. Evidently a change was taking place on the frontier. This new Ajax Overland outfit wanted whole hog or none. He'd noticed this same attitude on the part of the other Ajax trail crews they'd passed. They had not been friendly; they were new men, new teamsters, new wagonmasters. They did not know the old ways—the ways of friendliness on the trail, the helping hand to a rival outfit when necessary.

Thinking about these changes, Kern had the strange feeling that possibly it was better Uncle Billy McCloud had passed away. These new tactics, and this coldblooded approach to the freighting trade, would not have gone well with him.

"We'll hold up on that bluff ahead," Kern said. "I'll eat and then push on."

"Kind of anxious to see what's going on in Nebraska City?" Green asked him.

"A lot to be done," Kern told him.

An hour later he rode away from the camp. Moving at a fairly fast pace he could be in Nebraska City before dark. He rode a big black with a white face, one of the extra mounts he'd kept with the trail stock. The black was fresh and strong, and anxious to run. For almost an hour Kern kept the animal moving at a fast pace before stopping to wind her.

He passed Rock Springs, one of the stopping places along the trail, noticing that the water was quite low and very brackish. They could camp here tonight with the wagons, but the knowledge that the water was poor in the springs would have enabled them to stop a few miles back along Silver Creek. The Ajax wagonmaster had deliberately withheld this information out of spite.

At five o'clock in the afternoon Kern was about three miles from Nebraska City, already passing small cabins and huts in which lived remnants of the Delawares, a rather dirty, disreputable race of Indians that had deteriorated into a band of beggars. Many of them hung around Nebraska City, getting drunk when they could get the liquor, begging, scavenging, making themselves general nuisances.

The trail ran past their dwellings, and half-naked children came out of the huts to stare at him as he went by. Old men sat in the shade, smoking pipes, staring at nothing in particular. In the corral behind one hovel Kern saw two fairly good horses, and he wondered from whom they had been stolen.

He was a mile from Nebraska City, riding along

the edge of the dusty trail so as not to kick up too much dust, when he heard a sharp scream from a point about a hundred yards to the north. It was the scream of a woman.

Pulling up abruptly, Kern listened, wondering if it could be a Delaware squaw having trouble with her drunken husband. Then the woman screamed again. Jerking the black's head around, he sent the animal tearing in the direction of the scream. He was positive a white woman had made that sound.

There was a slight rise ahead of him with a willow-bordered creek on the other side. The creek would be dried up at this season of the year. Kern shot up to the top of the rise and then down the other side.

Directly in front of him, and close by the willows along the creek, a girl in a green riding costume sat astride an iron-gray horse. A young Delaware buck was holding the horse at the head, and the gray was trying to tear away, snorting in terror at the smell of the Indian.

A second Indian was dancing around, trying to get at the girl on the horse. She was beating at him with her riding whip, at the same time screaming for help.

None of them saw Kern as he shot over the rise and tore down at them. He came at a full gallop, coming up behind the fellow who was holding the horse. Hooking the Indian around the neck with his left arm, he dragged the man about twenty yards before coming to a stop and letting him drop to the ground.

The second Indian darted away toward the willows, and Kern helped him along with a shot from his Colt gun. Both of them disappeared into the willows, scurrying like a pair of frightened rabbits. They'd been dressed in white men's cast-off clothing, indescribably dirty.

Kern turned to the girl. She was slender, with honey-colored hair done in a bun at the back. The fright was still in her violet-blue eyes. From her riding habit he could tell that she was from the East. Very few of the girls in Nebraska City did any riding, and those that did, like Jennifer Steele, would not wear outfits like this.

Kern said, "You all right now, ma'am?"

"I'm all right," she gasped. "I—I'm glad you came along."

"They were after your horse," Kern told her. "The Delawares are noted horse-stealers. I wouldn't advise you to ride around alone and unarmed in this part of the country."

"I assure you it won't happen again." The girl laughed nervously. "I've only been in Nebraska City a week or so, and I was tired of doing nothing. I hired this horse and came up the trail a way."

"You're from the East?" Kern asked.

They'd turned their mounts and were moving

up the rise back to the clearly defined ox trail out of Nebraska City.

"We came from Baltimore," the light-haired girl told him. "My uncle, Colonel Paxton, wanted to see the West. I made him bring me along."

Kern learned more as they rode along. The girl's name was Daphne Paxton. She was the Colonel's niece and ward, having no parents of her own. She'd lived with the Colonel since she was ten years old. They'd lived in Baltimore and in other cities.

"How do you like Nebraska City?" Kern asked her. "It's not Baltimore."

"I love it," Daphne grinned. "It's exciting."

"Like this afternoon," Kern smiled. "I wouldn't advise you to get into this kind of scrape again."

They were coming into Nebraska City now, along the long, wide main street running down to the Missouri wharves. Dust lay in the street eight and ten inches deep. Dust from passing ox trains and other vehicles covered everything.

Passing by the new Ajax yards, Kern looked at them with interest, noting the long lines of new wagons, the pole corral with dozens of big bulls in the enclosure.

A third wagon shed was going up at one end of the yard, and workmen were still hammering on it even though it was past six o'clock in the evening. The Ajax yard dwarfed every other freighting yard in town. The Rocky Mountain

Freighting Company yard would have been lost inside this big enclosure. Piles of wagon tongues and axles lay in the yard, drying out, ready for use when needed. There was a big arch over the entranceway, all of it freshly painted new wood. Ajax Overland had come here to stay.

As they moved past the office, located a short distance down from the arch, a man in a brown coat and brown broad-rimmed hat came out. He was not a big man, but he had the widest shoulders Kern Harlan had ever seen in his life. He was smoking a slender Mexican cigarillo, and he glanced over at them as they rode by.

Daphne Paxton lifted a gloved hand to him and smiled. The man with the broad shoulders nodded and smiled back. He had a wide, smooth face to go with those shoulders, and a pair of cool green eyes. He stood there for a moment, one hand resting on the handrail outside the door, the cigarillo in his mouth, coolly studying Kern.

When they were past Kern said idly, "An Ajax Overland man?"

"I thought you knew him," Miss Paxton chirped. "That was Mr. Trace Bovard, head of Ajax. Uncle and I met him our first day in town. He's an interesting man."

"Is he?" Kern murmured, and he wondered why the remark should annoy him. He didn't look back at Trace Bovard as they rode into the main part of town. The Rocky Mountain Freighting yard was on the other side of town, nearer to the water, and he had to go all the way through town to reach it.

Daphne Paxton was saying, "You say you've just come in from Denver, Mr.—?"

"Harlan," Kern said briefly. "Kern Harlan. I'm with Rocky Mountain Freighting."

He felt the girl looking at him curiously as they rode along. Then she said, "You're Mr. McCloud's ward, aren't you?"

"That's right," Kern nodded, and the pain came back more poignantly than ever. This was Uncle Billy McCloud's town he was riding into. Uncle Billy had been here when Nebraska City consisted of a dozen shacks and a single wharf large enough to dock one river steamer. There were probably fifty or sixty boats tied up along the spacious wharves now, unloading into the lines of high-sided freight wagons that would haul the cargos to the interior.

"We're all very sorry about Mr. McCloud," Miss Paxton murmured. "He seemed like a very fine man."

"They didn't breed them any better on the border," Kern told her. "He was aces high."

Men along the street who knew him waved as he went by, and he nodded back. Most of his acquaintances were freighting men with different freight outfits, friendly rivals of Rocky Mountain. He sensed there was a difference in this town now. Much of the friendliness seemed to have gone out of it. It had grown up in the short time he'd been away. New buildings were being constructed. The stage office had been greatly enlarged to accommodate the increased traffic to points west. There were more saloons, more gambling houses, more warehouses and stores. There was even another church up one of the side streets. But these things did not make the difference.

There was a new atmosphere here. Nebraska City was no longer the small town on the river. It was becoming a big city; there was already the feeling of coldness that he'd noticed on the trail when they passed Ajax Overland outfits. The town was full of strangers.

"We're staying at the Sherman Hotel," Daphne Paxton told him. "I'd like you to meet Uncle."

Kern nodded. The Sherman was on the next block, and Colonel Tobias Paxton was sitting in a wicker chair on the spacious porch when they came up. He was smoking an expensive cigar, a portly, round-faced man with graying hair and a short gray beard. His eyes were bland and blue, showing interest as he looked at Kern. There was a distinct trace of the South in his accent as he spoke.

He said, "Pleasure to meet you, Mr. Harlan. We've heard much about your abilities as a wagonmaster in this pleasant city."

"Mr. Harlan rescued me from two Delaware Indians who tried to steal my horse," Daphne told him. "I don't know what would have happened if he hadn't come along."

"My dear," Tobias Paxton said pompously, "you should never ride alone in this country." Turning to Kern he said, "We are highly indebted to you, sir."

"My pleasure," Kern murmured. He was anxious to reach the Rocky Mountain office now. There was much to be done, many things to be straightened out. He said, "We'll have a drink tonight, Colonel."

"I shall look forward to it," Colonel Paxton smiled.

Riding away from the porch, Kern found himself wondering about the man. He didn't quite get the Colonel. Paxton acted more friendly than was usual on a first meeting, but perhaps that could be attributed to his Southern background.

Kern dismissed the man from his mind, but he couldn't quite dismiss Daphne Paxton of the honey-colored hair and sky-blue eyes. The thought suddenly came to him that Miss Paxton had no Southern accent at all, and this was strange, considering that she'd been brought up by the Colonel.

Riding into the Rocky Mountain yards, Kern was greeted on all sides by Rocky Mountain employees. Yardmen, teamsters, blacksmiths, finishing the day's work, came out of the sheds to shake hands with him.

He was chatting amiably with big Tom Moran, one of the teamsters, when Burton Reeves, the office superintendent, called from the door, "Miss Jennifer Steele to see you, Harlan."

Chapter Three

Walking toward the office door, Kern knew why Jennifer Steele had come. Having known Uncle Billy McCloud from childhood up, she had to come over and pay her respects. She wasn't coming out of any personal wish to see him, because they'd never got along.

He was remembering the time when she'd been nine years old and he'd been seventeen and he'd threatened to take her across his knee and spank her. She'd been making a nuisance of herself in the Rocky Mountain yards. And she didn't seem to have grown up much since then. She went out on the trail with her brother's wagons, and she handled a blacksnake whip nearly as well as some of the bullwhackers Jack Steele employed. She dressed like a man, too, which was unnatural. Kern Harlan liked to see a woman dress like a woman—the way Daphne Paxton had been dressed, for instance. He had to smile, comparing the two, because there was no comparison.

Reeves, the office superintendent, waited for him at the door and greeted him perfunctorily, as if he'd just been down the street for a drink instead of to Denver on a two-month trip through Indian country.

Reeves, thin, with lank brown hair and a

drooping mouth, said rather coldly, "Guess she saw you riding in, Harlan. She's inside."

"How are you?" Kern asked him, knowing that the man resented the fact that he'd gone into the yards to greet the yardmen before coming into the office. Burton Reeves had been with Rocky Mountain for quite a few years. He was an able, efficient man in the office, and Billy McCloud, in his declining years, had turned over much of the work to him, with Kern taking over the outside work—the making up of the outfits, the care of the wagons, the buying of new stock, the hiring of men.

Reeves resented him, too, knowing that Billy McCloud intended to pass on to his ward everything he owned. Uncle Billy had said that on many occasions; his will had been made out to that effect, and Kern, when the news came to him of Uncle Billy's death, was aware of the fact that he now owned Rocky Mountain Freighting, lock, stock, and barrel.

"Glad to see you back," Reeves said, and his voice was still a trifle cold. He had long, slender white hands, always stained with ink, and slate-colored eyes that were constantly shifting.

Jennifer Steele was in the outer office, and Kern passed on through the door from the inside office, closing it behind him. She sat up on the counter the way he expected that she would, heels kicking the pine boards, head down—the same worn, blue Levi's, a faded but clean gray flannel shirt, scuffed boots, and a black, flat-crowned sombrero.

She had black hair and hazel eyes, with always a kind of defiant look in them, especially when she looked at him. The oil lamp had been lighted in the office as dusk came, and she looked a little different in this light. She'd changed, too, like the city, but Kern Harlan was not sure in what way.

He remembered now that he hadn't seen her in more than six months. She'd gone down to St. Louis the previous winter with her brother, and a short while before they were due back Kern had taken the Denver Trail with his bull outfit. She'd grown some in that brief period of time.

He said, "How are you, Jennifer?"

She nodded, but she didn't get off the counter. She sat there like a small girl, kicking her heels lightly against the wood, just the way she'd done many, many years before when she'd come in to chat with Uncle Billy McCloud.

"Sorry about Uncle Billy," she said.

Kern sat down on a chair across the room. She was older, more mature. Some of the wildness seemed to have left her, and she'd been wild in her early teens. She'd made no bones about the fact that she'd disliked him, too. He'd told her off a number of times—once in front of the whole grinning yard crew, when she'd tried to break in a new team of his oxen on a bet with one of the bullwhackers, and a valuable bull had come out of it with a broken leg.

Kern said, "Tell me about it." He paused and then he said, "It was his heart, wasn't it?"

"He came in from the yard one afternoon," Jennifer told him. "It was a pretty hot day. I had just come into the office to see him about a few wagons Jack wanted to rent for a trip to Fort Wilson. He collapsed in his chair."

"You were with him, then," Kern murmured, "when he died."

"I got Doc Wharton in," Jennifer said, "but Uncle Billy didn't last long."

Kern moistened his lips. "He have anything to say?" he asked.

Jennifer looked at him, and then at the floor again. She frowned a little. "Told me to say good-by to you," she said. "To take care of yourself."

Kern nodded. He was noting the way the light played around the edges of her dark hair. He'd never noticed her hair before. He said, changing the subject, "Been some changes in Nebraska City. That new Ajax outfit."

He saw her eyes get a trifle harder. "They're big," she said, "and they're growing all the time. They bought out Pioneer a few weeks ago. They also bought out, or forced out, Ben Alton's Great Western line."

"Forced out?" Kern asked.

"That's about the size of it," Jennifer told him bitterly. "They're big and they're rough, and they don't play the game the way we do."

"How can they force a man to sell out?" Kern asked curiously.

"Underbid him on contracts," Jennifer said tersely, "for one thing. Pay his teamsters and yardmen to come over to their side of the fence so he can't put an outfit on the road even if he does get a contract. That's what they did with poor Ben. He went downriver to St. Louis yesterday. He's through."

Kern rolled a cigarette thoughtfully. "That's news," he admitted. "Bovard the chap runs Ajax?"

"Trace Bovard," Jennifer nodded. "He'll be after you, Kern. He's already after Jack. Offered to buy us out last week—at about half what we're worth. Jack laughed at his man."

"So he'll be after me," Kern murmured.

"Somebody else after you, too," Jennifer said. "Bull Shannon heard you were due in any day. He's been talking. You'll have to have it out with him someday, Kern."

Kern nodded casually. "I'll have it out," he said.

Shannon was a giant bullwhacker who fancied himself the top fighting man in Nebraska City. The previous spring Kern had thrashed, badly, a supposedly rough fighter from the Pioneer yards, and the talk and conjecture had begun as to who would come out best if Kern and Bull Shannon crossed. Evidently Shannon was curious, too, and his pride was getting the best of him.

"If you want to see where Uncle Billy is buried," Jennifer said, "we can ride out tomorrow morning."

"Like to," Kern told her. "Thanks for taking care of things."

"We all liked Uncle Billy," Jennifer murmured. She slipped off the counter and walked across the room, not tall, but lithe, with the movements of a cat, so unlike Daphne Paxton.

"Good to get home again," Kern stated, and for some reason he was not anxious for her to go. A short time before she'd annoyed him; he'd seen her around all the time, and she'd been in his hair. In six months there had been a change. She couldn't have grown up in six months, but yet there was a very definite change in her. The coltishness, the awkwardness seemed to have disappeared, and she was a woman.

Jennifer Steele said coolly, "You've done pretty well in the short time you've been home, Kern."

Kern looked at her as he lighted a cigarette. "What does that mean?" he asked.

"Funny thing," Jennifer said acidly, "how a woman happens to be riding alone out on the trail just when Kern Harlan's bull outfit is due in.

Everybody in town knows your wagons will be in tomorrow, and everyone figured you'd probably be coming in ahead of them late this afternoon."

Kern grinned. "You think Miss Paxton was waiting for me along the trail?" he asked.

"Why not?" Jennifer snapped. "Every woman's waiting for a man."

Kern looked at her through the tobacco smoke. "How about you, Jennifer?" he asked.

"I'm waiting, too," she said thinly, "but it has to be a man."

She went out then, closing the door a little louder than was necessary. Kern sat there in the chair, smoking, looking at the door. She was undoubtedly wrong about Daphne Paxton waiting for him out on the trail. To begin with, Miss Paxton didn't know him from Adam, and besides, there was the matter of the Delawares. The beggarly Indians, of course, could have been hired for that job, but it was ridiculous. A girl like Daphne Paxton did not go out of her way to meet a man. There were a hundred men in Nebraska City whom she could have for the asking, and there was only one Daphne Paxton.

Burton Reeves came in, a batch of papers in his hand. He said, "Jason Dow will want to see you, Harlan. He handled all the legal matters. He has the will."

Kern nodded. Dow was the attorney for Rocky Mountain Freighting, and a close friend of Uncle

Billy's. He would have to see Dow first, and find out exactly where he stood.

Reeves cleared his throat, thumbed through the papers, and said, "You'll be running Rocky Mountain from now on, Harlan. Will there be any changes here?"

"What do you mean?" Kern asked him.

"As far as I'm concerned," Reeves said bluntly. "Do you want me to run the office the same as usual?"

"You were good enough for Uncle Billy," Kern observed. "That's good enough for me."

Burton Reeves nodded. He said, "Thanks, Harlan." Then he went out, and Kern stared after him, frowning a little, wondering about the man. Reeves had always been the close-mouthed type, never too friendly, keeping to himself, harboring his own small grudges, if he had any. It was hard to say what a man like Burton Reeves had inside his head. Possibly it was nothing, and then again it could be much.

Getting up, Kern went into Uncle Billy's office, which was now his own office. He looked at Uncle Billy's battered swivel chair and the old oak desk. Then he went over to the window and looked out across the darkened Rocky Mountain yard. The Missouri ran past the yard, and he could see the lights of river packets tied up along the wharves.

A side-wheeler was unloading under the light of

flaming torches, and he watched the roustabouts moving up and down the planks, carrying barrels, boxes, sacks, piling the supplies on the wharf, covering them with huge tarpaulins.

He could smell the river as it flowed sluggishly past the city, heavy with sand, with floating debris carried down from the upper river. The old, familiar sounds of this sprawling river town came to his ears—the shouts and yells of the roustabouts, the bells of a packet moving into a berth along the wharf, the singing in a nearby saloon, and then a drunk stumbling down along the picket fence enclosing the Rocky Mountain yard, cursing as he walked, cursing aimlessly, futilely.

This was Uncle Billy McCloud's town, and it had been a nice town—one that Billy McCloud loved. He, Kern Harlan, wanted to see it remain that way. This was the hub of the wheel. Out from Nebraska City—to the north, to the south, and particularly to the west—rolled the big freight wagons, the life line of the frontier, bringing the machinery for the mines, the plows for the farmers, the wagons, the tools, the foods they could not grow, the manufactured goods, the clothing. The big wagons made life possible west of Nebraska City; the stumbling oxen, crawling over Indian-infested plains, stupid and dull and incredibly strong, were the lifeblood of the frontier.

In the semidarkness, coming up from the wharves, moving past the Rocky Mountain yard, were a half-dozen big Murphy wagons. They were already loaded, the tarpaulins lashed down across the loads, and across each tarpaulin were scrawled the words in foot-high letters, "Ajax Overland."

Kern's lips tightened a little as he watched the big wagons rumble by, and heard the wheels creaking, the rattle of the yokes, and the unintelligible cries of the bullwhackers striding beside the wagons. These wagons were going up to the Ajax yards, and probably moving out at dawn tomorrow.

Everywhere you looked it was Ajax—on the trail, in the town, in the talk of the people. The big Ajax Overland outfit seemed to be gradually drawing a noose around the neck of the freighting business, reaching out to absorb all the other companies, trying to buy them out, trying to force them out, as Jennifer Steele had intimated.

He remembered as a boy complaining to Uncle Billy that there were too many freighting companies in Nebraska City, too much competition, and Billy McCloud's sage remark:

"When the competition ends, boy, Nebraska City will die. When one outfit gains control of all traffic, it'll be hell for the people who depend upon us out there."

He'd pointed a gnarled hand out across the

vast stretches of open country to the west—to Denver, to the dozens of Army posts, to the little settlements springing up everywhere, to the isolated ranchers and settlers who depended upon the big freight wagons.

"Someday," Uncle Billy had said, "the railroads will come out here, Kern, but now they must depend upon us. Keep those wagons rolling, boy."

Later, as he grew older, he knew what Uncle Billy meant about one outfit gaining control of all traffic. The freighting company that controlled the traffic and did all the hauling out of Nebraska City also controlled the rates. Instead of charging a dollar per hundred pounds per hundred miles, they could charge three, five, ten! They could let cargos rust or rot on the wharves until the consignees agreed to pay what they asked. They could bleed the country to death.

Kern turned away from the window. As he went outside to the street, Tom Moran, one of his teamsters, came up and said, "Figured I'd tell you, Kern. Bull Shannon is puttin' up a hundred dollars to any man that'll take it that he kin whip you if you got enough nerve to stand up agin him."

Kern smiled a little. "Thanks, Tom," he said.

"He's talkin' big," Moran murmured, "an' he's a big man, Kern."

"I know," Kern nodded. "I'll watch him, Tom."

"Another thing," Moran said. "Most o' the boys in this yard have been workin' for Billy McCloud for a long time. We kind o' hated to see him go, but we figure we got another good man in his place. There ain't nobody goin' over to Ajax Overland."

Kern looked at him. "Ajax Overland?" he repeated.

"Feller was in here two days ago," Moran said, "offerin' the boys forty dollars a month instead o' the thirty we been gettin' from Rocky Mountain. Reckon we're all stayin' with you, Kern."

Kern nodded, but there was a glint in his eyes. He said, "You won't regret it, Tom."

That was another thing Uncle Billy had mentioned. When one outfit got control of the trade, they controlled wages as well as rates. Ajax could pay teamsters extra money now, and then take it away from them later when they'd absorbed all the other outfits, and every teamster and yardman had to take the money Ajax offered or not work at all. Ajax could pay twenty dollars a month then, and the bullwhackers could take it or leave it.

"Hell with the money," Tom Moran said. "We like pushin' them wagons for Rocky Mountain, Kern." He went on down the street, and Kern saw him step into the first saloon he came to.

Instead of going directly to the lawyer Dow's office, Kern went back into his own office. He opened the door to the little cubbyhole of a room where Burton Reeves was working overtime, and he said, "Starting tomorrow, Reeves, we're paying our bullwhackers and yardmen forty dollars a month instead of thirty."

Reeves looked at him and licked his thin lips. His face was expressionless. He said, "That'll only be so much more liquor they can buy, Harlan. Besides, our overhead is already quite stiff."

"We'll make it up," Kern told him. "We'll get more orders; we'll put more outfits on the road."

Reeves nodded, but he didn't say anything, and Kern had the queer feeling that the man was laughing at him. He closed the door and went out into the street again, walking west toward the house that Billy McCloud had built years ago, and in which he'd been raised when McCloud picked him up in the Nebraska City streets, a homeless waif, his emigrant parents dead from mountain fever.

He had many things on his mind as he walked down the familiar street. There were Ajax Overland and Bull Shannon and Reeves and Jennifer Steele and Daphne Paxton, and especially Daphne Paxton.

Chapter Four

Amos Scott, the old colored man who kept house for Billy McCloud, let him in, grinning broadly, shaking his hand. The house was big, the biggest in town, two stories high with a front porch and an overhead balcony.

Kern Harlan went through the main dining room, underneath the huge cut-glass chandelier, which had awed him as a boy. He went up the stairs, the winding mahogany and white staircase, and he remembered sliding down this banister, and Uncle Billy catching him at the bottom, laughing.

It was a big house, a lonely house with Uncle Billy gone. Kern changed his clothes after taking a hot bath in the water Amos had prepared for him. He ate in the kitchen with old Amos watching him approvingly, rubbing his black hands.

At eight-thirty, dressed in a clean black coat, cleanshaven, he went down to Jason Dow's house. Dow, like Uncle Billy, was an old man, small, shriveled, almost bald, with bright blue eyes like a bird. He said:

"Come in, come in, Kern. Heard you'd just arrived."

Kern shook hands with him.

"A few formalities to get over with," Dow said busily. "Some papers to sign. Terrible thing about Uncle Billy. Terrible thing. He left everything to you, of course, house, business, what money there was."

Kern looked at him. "What money there was?" he repeated.

"Not too much of it," Dow said carefully. "I've gone over his books with Mr. Reeves. You know Uncle Billy was not too good a businessman; he didn't have the hard head that makes for success."

Kern nodded, thinking of all the men who owed Uncle Billy money, of all the debts Billy McCloud had erased from his books and from his memory. It was logical that Rocky Mountain Freighting would not be on too sound a financial basis with a man like Uncle Billy at the helm.

"Just a few papers to sign to make it legal," Jason Dow hummed. He fumbled through the papers and he added, "A little tight for most freighting men in this town since Ajax Overland opened business. Heard of Ajax, Kern?"

"I've heard of it," Kern said dryly.

"That Trace Bovard wants whole hog or none," Dow scowled. "A businessman, a hard businessman, Kern. He'll make an offer to you for Rocky Mountain. He's made just about every freighting man in town an offer for his business."

"And if they won't sell," Kern murmured, "he forces them out. Is that right?"

"That's what they tell me," Dow nodded. "You intend to keep Rocky Mountain, Kern?"

"I'll keep it," Kern said slowly, "until the railroads come, and then I'll buy a railroad."

He left Dow's residence an hour later, walking back to the main part of town. At this hour Nebraska City was coming to life. All the freight yards were empty, and half the teamsters and yardmen in town seemed to have congregated in the dozens of saloons and gambling houses along the street.

As he was passing the Double Yoke Saloon, Tobias Paxton hailed him from the porch. Beyond Paxton, standing at the bar of the saloon, chatting with another man, was Trace Bovard, head of Ajax Overland. Kern went up the steps.

Paxton said to him, "Waiting for you, Mr. Harlan. Come inside."

Kern Harlan wondered whether Paxton's niece had been waiting for him, too, the way Jennifer Steele had suggested.

Pushing through the batwing doors, he had his first good look at Trace Bovard at the bar. Bovard's smooth face was shining in the light of the overhead lamps. He wore a brown suit and he did not carry a gun, which was rather unusual in this town.

He'd seen Kern coming through the door, and his green eyes shifted slightly as he spoke to his companion at the bar. He had a prow of a nose, and the hand holding the liquor glass was smooth and hairless, like his face. A gold watch chain dangled from his vest. His boots and clothing were the best; the hat he wore was new, brown in color.

Tobias Paxton was saying jovially, "Heard a great deal about you, Mr. Harlan. Best wagon-master in Nebraska City. They say you can talk the language of the bulls you drive."

They were moving past Trace Bovard as Paxton spoke, and Bovard smiled and nodded to Paxton.

"Owner of Ajax Overland," Paxton breezed when they pulled up to an empty space at the crowded bar. "You've met Mr. Bovard?"

"Heard of him," Kern said dryly.

"Very successful," Paxton told him. "You should know him, Mr. Harlan. Both in the same business."

"From what I understand," Kern observed, "Mr. Bovard is quite anxious to be in the business alone."

Paxton laughed. "He is known as a sharp competitor," he admitted. He poured two drinks from the bottle the bartender shoved in front of them, and he said, "Your health, sir."

Kern nodded and lifted his glass. He saw Bull Shannon coming through the door then, about a dozen bullwhackers behind him, grinning, half-drunken men, nearly tearing the doors from the hinges as they came in.

Shannon was a giant of a man, thick in the neck, in the shoulders, in the waist. He was hatless, and his hair was a red fuzz on the top of his head. He had huge forearms, as big as the average man's thighs, and his fingers were thick and stubby, covered with the same red fuzz as his head.

He'd been drinking, possibly heavily, but it did not show in the way he walked. His face shone more than usual, and his pale blue eyes were lighter in color.

Harlan had seen the big man around town many times, and he'd passed some Pioneer outfits with Shannon handling one of the wagons. He wondered now if the giant had gone over to Ajax Overland.

Shannon hauled up at the bar a few yards from Kern and Paxton. The crowd with him elbowed other drinkers out of line roughly. There was a lot of laughing and joking, along with the usual horseplay. Kern sipped his drink, smiled calmly, and waited for Shannon to make his play. He knew that it was coming. It had to come, because the Bull had made remarks and he had to back them up now.

The bartender came over and said softly, "You want me to send for some Rocky Mountain boys, Kern?"

Kern shook his head. "I'm all right," he said.

"Lot o' that crowd here," the bartender murmured.

"Just one going to fight," Kern smiled.

Tobias Paxton had overheard the remark, and he said quickly, "Fight! Who's going to fight, Mr. Harlan?"

"I am," Kern said calmly.

With that he pushed away from the bar and walked easily up to Bull Shannon. The men near Shannon stopped talking suddenly, and the big man spun around as if he expected to be hit.

Harlan smiled at him. He said, "Bull, I'll be waiting outside for you. I'll wait five minutes. If you don't come before then, don't ever come."

Bull Shannon stared at him, mouth open in surprise. Kern nodded to him, turned around, and strolled toward the door whistling softly.

Outside, Kern walked down to the tie rack, took off his coat, and draped it across the bar. He placed his hat on top of the coat, and then started to roll up his sleeves. Behind him the crowd was pouring out on the porch, and the cry was going up and down the street, "Fight! Fight!"

Turning around, Kern leaned back against the tie rack, the light from the saloon revealing him clearly. He looked bigger with his coat off. He was six feet tall, and he was built solidly, proportionately, not too much weight around the stomach. He'd taken off his string tie and opened his white shirt collar, revealing his neck, strongly corded, supple.

Men tumbled out of saloon doors on either

side of the street and came up toward the Double Yoke. Flares were brought out, held high in the air, illuminating the wide road from one side of the street to the other.

Bull Shannon came out on the porch, towering head and shoulders above the others, looking a little sheepish. A man yelled from across the road, "There's your meat, Bull. Eat him up!"

Bull Shannon grinned. He looked at Kern, who was smiling up at him coolly, and then he looked away. He was a little puzzled, and the seed of doubt had been planted in his mind the way Kern wanted it planted. Usually Bull Shannon won his fights before the first punch was struck. Tonight it was not going to be so.

Shannon came down to the bottom step, rubbed his flattened nose thoughtfully, and said, "You lookin' for trouble, Harlan?"

"That's right," Kern smiled. "Come and get it, Bull."

He wasn't afraid of this big man, despite Shannon's enormous strength. He'd had his fights in his early days in the Rocky Mountain yard, and he knew how to handle himself. In addition to that, he'd had a professional bare-fist pugilist working as a blacksmith in the yard for six months a number of years ago, and he'd boxed with the man nearly every evening, learning this trade. He'd become fairly proficient before the blacksmith moved on westward.

He knew that he could move around much faster than Bull, and that he struck a punch just as hard as Shannon because he knew how to hit with his fists, getting maximum power out of short, jolting blows, where the fighter of Shannon's type bludgeoned the other man. Shannon had too much weight around his waist to begin with, and tonight he'd been drinking, which would not help him when the going got rough.

Jack Steele, Jennifer's brother, and a fighter of note himself, came up and said, "I'll see to it that nobody else jumps you, Kern."

He was almost as big as Shannon, a golden-haired man in his late thirties, a smiling, blue-eyed giant whom Kern had always liked and respected.

Kern said, "Thanks, Jack. I'll appreciate that."

"You want him now?" Steele asked. "You just came in off the trail, Kern. You've been on a horse most of the day."

"I'll ride another one tonight," Kern chuckled. "Don't worry, Jack." He saw Jennifer up on the walk, her hands shoved in her back pockets, a frown on her face. She made no move to leave when Shannon pushed through the crowd in front of him and walked down to the tie rail.

Kern still stood with his arms draped across the tie rail, smiling pleasantly at Shannon. Behind him he could hear the crowd gathering, the hum of excitement. More flaring torches were brought up to give them light, and a big circle was left in the middle of the road.

Shannon rubbed his hands together, rubbed his jaws, and then suddenly drove forward, lunging like a huge bear. He had more speed than Kern had expected from a man carrying so much weight.

Ducking under his charge, Kern rammed a left fist into his stomach. It felt as if he were driving his fist into a sack of grain. Bull Shannon grunted, pulled up, and grinned.

Kern slipped under the tie rail and out into the circle that had been formed for them. Shannon suddenly tore in again, hitting the tie rack with his stomach, ripping it from its moorings, and stumbling over it, raining ponderous blows at Kern's face as he came forward.

One punch caught Kern on the side of the jaw and he went down as if he'd been axed. He rolled as he hit the dust, and then he came up again, his cheek slashed by the punch, blood dripping down his chin. He was still smiling. Shannon had made no move to pile on top of him when he went down, which was a nice gesture. It was going to be a clean fight.

"All right," Kern said. "All right, Bull."

"Don't fight too long," Shannon warned him. "I'll rip you up, Harlan."

Kern grinned at him. He circled around, hands held high, watching for his openings, and then he was in very fast, his left fist driving into Shannon's mouth, pulverizing the lips. He hit twice more before Shannon could get off one of his swings.

When the big man missed by many inches, Kern was in again, ripping punches into the stomach, actually driving Shannon back a few paces this time, and the crowd howled.

Jack Steele circled around them, keeping the crowd back, pushing one man in the face with a huge hand when the spectator came too close to them, always smiling, a pleasant man.

As Kern moved around in front of Shannon, seeking for another opening, he saw Trace Bovard up on the walk, a cigar in his mouth, hands hooked in his vest pockets, watching. Tobias Paxton stood a short distance behind him, up on the porch steps, leaning forward.

Bull Shannon came in again, head lowered, the blood pouring from his cut mouth, and Kern hit him twice in the face, shifting away from Shannon's charge. He kept moving, to the right and to the left, never giving the giant a stationary target to hit at.

Shannon plodded after him, very patient, taking the vicious punches calmly, always coming in. He nearly caught Kern with a terrific swing on one occasion after he'd backed him into the crowd across the road from the Double Yoke. The blow landed high on the head, glancing off. Kern staggered a little, righted himself, and moved away again.

He didn't move away all the time. When Shannon stopped chasing him, Kern suddenly darted in with a fusillade of blows. On one occasion he drove the Bull back against the broken tie rail, and Shannon fell back over it, landing with a terrific thud.

He got up, dusted himself off, rubbed his hands on his pants, and came in again. His face was beginning to resemble a piece of raw meat as Kern continued to pound it from long range. The straight, fast punches Kern threw at him constantly put Shannon off balance so that he could not launch his own wild swings.

The watching crowd became silent after a while. Only the sound of the blows could be heard, solid, sickening, as Kern's fists collided with Shannon's face.

The giant went down to his knees after one heavy onslaught, and he got up slowly, blood in his eyes now from the cuts up high. He came in, and Kern hit him in the stomach. He was stumbling, shaking his head to clear the fog out of his mind.

Kern watched him, knowing that he had to knock the giant unconscious before he would stop fighting, not liking the business now. He respected the big man for the way he'd fought tonight. It had been a clean, hard fight, with the

Bull always driving in, refusing to take advantage of his tremendous weight and close with Kern in a wrestling match.

Again and again Kern knocked him down, but he got up again, staggering forward, swinging, unable to see his man now, walking into the blows, grunting. Watching him, Kern had the feeling that this could go on all night. He looked at Jack Steele, and Steele nodded.

Walking in between the fighters, Steele grasped Bull Shannon, pinioning his arms to his side. He started to talk to the giant soothingly, holding him so that he could not move. Kern heard him say, "All right, Bull. That's all now. That's all."

Shannon rumbled something in his throat and kept pushing in. Steele had to dig his heels into the dust to hold him, and it took several minutes before Shannon gave up his efforts to break away and continue the fight.

The crowd closed in around them, some of the Rocky Mountain men who'd been in the crowd pounding Kern's back gleefully, holding up their winnings. Two of them had Kern by the arms and were pulling him forcibly into the bar to buy him a drink.

He went with them, although he would have felt better if he could have fallen down on a cot and lain there. The fight had lasted for fully thirty minutes, and his arms were weary from hitting at Shannon. He'd taken dozens of blows on the arms and forearms, protecting himself, and he'd been hit in the body and in the face. He was still bleeding from the gash on his cheek, and he held a handkerchief to it as he went up the steps to the porch.

Looking back, he noticed that Bull Shannon had broken away from Jack Steele and was walking stolidly up the street, away from the Double Yoke Saloon, walking alone now, his head down, feeling his way along the line of buildings. He knew how Shannon felt. The giant had fancied himself the toughest fighting man in Nebraska City. He would have to revise his thinking now.

At the Double Yoke bar Tobias Paxton came up with Trace Bovard. He said to Kern, "Mr. Harlan, meet Mr. Bovard of Ajax Overland."

Kern looked at the Ajax owner. He shook Bovard's hand, but there was no smile on his face, no warmth in his eyes.

Bovard said to him, "You're quite a fighting man, Mr. Harlan. I had ten dollars on Shannon. I evidently picked the wrong man."

He had a soft, purring voice, and his green eyes narrowed into a smile as he spoke. His handshake was strong.

Kern said casually, "You should know your men before you bet on them, Mr. Bovard."

"True," Bovard acknowledged. "May I buy you a drink, Harlan?"

"Had mine for the evening," Kern told him. "Thanks."

Trace Bovard nodded and smiled. He ordered drinks for himself and for Paxton, and then he said, "Very unfortunate your losing your uncle, Mr. Harlan. I didn't know Billy McCloud, but I've heard much about him."

"I was Billy McCloud's ward," Kern corrected him. "We were not blood relations."

Bovard lifted his eyebrows slightly in surprise. "I was not aware of that fact," he murmured. "You are the present owner of Rocky Mountain Freighting?"

"I inherited it," Kern said briefly. He daubed at his cut face with the handkerchief, offering no more information.

"I understand," Trace Bovard went on smoothly, "that you are just in off the trail, Mr. Harlan. How did you find it?"

Kern looked at him. "Fair," he said.

"Indian troubles?" Bovard wanted to know.

"Not that I know of," Kern said.

Bovard laughed deep down in his chest. He said, "You are not too communicative, Mr. Harlan."

Kern regarded him coolly. "I learned that from Ajax wagonmasters on the trail," he stated. "You should hire men, Mr. Bovard, who are civil. In Nebraska City we have been accustomed to that."

Trace Bovard lifted his glass to the light and

squinted at it thoughtfully. "Nebraska City is a frontier town," he murmured. "I was not aware that civility was one of its attributes."

"You have a lot to learn about Nebraska City," Kern retorted, "if you intend to stay in business here, Mr. Bovard."

Bovard smiled a little, and in that smile Kern Harlan read the strength of the man. He was hard, tough, ruthless.

Bovard said softly, "I intend to stay in business here, Mr. Harlan, and possibly a long time after many of the other freighting outfits have folded up."

"Folded up or been forced out," Kern said tersely.

"One and the same thing," Bovard observed, "and all in the way you look at it."

"I'll look at it this way." Kern smiled grimly, turning to face him now. "The next Ajax man who comes into my yard offering higher wages to my yardmen will find himself at the bottom of the ox trough."

Trace Bovard put his empty glass down on the bar wood, and then shoved his hands in his vest pockets. He said, unperturbed, "You're rough with your fists, Harlan, and you're rough with your talk. I never liked rough men."

Tobias Paxton cut in from the side, protestingly, "Gentlemen, gentlemen, we're having a friendly drink here."

"I bear no ill will toward Rocky Mountain Freighting," Trace Bovard purred.

"I'll say the same about Ajax Overland," Kern said thinly, "when Ajax stays in its own yard."

"The man who stays in his own yard dies," Bovard chuckled. "That goes for a freight outfit, too."

Kern looked at him steadily. "There are other ways that a man or an outfit can die, Bovard, and that's by crowding someone else. In Nebraska City we don't like to be crowded."

He nodded briefly to Tobias Paxton and walked out of the saloon. Going through the door, he saw Jack Steele standing with another freighting man, and Steele called after him softly, "He can't bluff a good freighting man, can he, Kern?"

"Not in this world," Kern growled. He went down the street, knowing now that the lines were being drawn. Trace Bovard had told him quite bluntly what his intentions were in Nebraska City. He was going to expand; he was going to cut down every other freighter who got in his way. It was going to be a fight all along the line.

Moving past one of the smaller, drab little saloons at the far end of the town on the way back to the McCloud house, Kern spotted Bull Shannon sitting at a corner table, alone, a glass of liquor on the table in front of him. The Bull, face swollen hideously, sat there, looking at the liquor through eyes that were little more than slits.

Turning into the saloon, Kern walked directly to his table and sat down. Shannon stared at him uncertainly, his vision still blurred.

Kern said to him, "It's Kern Harlan, Bull. How do you feel?"

Shannon licked his puffed lips. "Bad," he said. "Bad, Harlan."

Kern smiled over at him. "Lucky thing," he said, "that Jack Steele stopped you, Bull."

Shannon looked at him, and then at the liquor glass again. He didn't say anything.

Kern said blandly, "I was finished, Bull. I couldn't have stood on my feet another minute."

Shannon blinked at him. "Hah!" he gulped.

"You had me whipped," Kern told him. "Steele knew that. He didn't want to see me hurt. He stopped it."

Bull Shannon was leaning forward in his chair, staring at him. He said slowly, uncertainly, "Sure—sure, Harlan."

"You're the best fighter in Nebraska City," Kern told him. "The best on the whole frontier. I've seen them."

Bull Shannon downed his drink. He rubbed his huge hands together, and some semblance of life came back to his eyes. He said thickly, "Me an' you, Harlan. We're the best. We can lick 'em all. Both of us."

"That's right," Kern nodded. "I'm hiring good bullwhackers at Rocky Mountain, Bull. They tell me you can handle a dozen wagons at once."

"Handle 'em all." Shannon laughed hoarsely. "I'm the best damn bull man there is, Harlan. I'll sign with you."

Kern clapped him on the back as he got up from the chair. He said, "We'll get along, Bull, and I can use men like you."

Out on the street again, as he walked toward his own house, the night was cool. The fight had helped to get something out of his system, and he felt better for it. He'd made a friend in Bull Shannon tonight, even if he'd made an enemy in Trace Bovard.

Then he wondered about Tobias Paxton. Daphne's uncle knew Bovard, but possibly they were just casual acquaintances. He wondered if there could be any connection between the two. There was the matter, also, of Daphne's being out on the trail late this afternoon for some reason or other. That undoubtedly was coincidental. There could be no reason why she should want to meet him. He was thinking on these things as he turned into his own quiet street.

Chapter Five

In the morning, still sore and stiff from the fight with Bull Shannon, Kern rode into the Steele Freighting yard. The yard was a scene of much activity. Big Murphy wagons were being greased and overhauled. A number of them were jacked up with new wagon axles being fitted.

In the bull corral several teams of oxen were being broken to the yoke, the bullwhackers swearing at the animals as they attempted to teach them how to work in harness.

Jack Steele came out of the blacksmith shop, a heavy hammer in his hand, his wide, handsome face smudged, smiling as usual. He lifted a big hand to Kern and said, "You're up early for a man who nearly took a bad licking last night."

Kern dismounted. He saw Jennifer coming out of the stable, leading a little bay mare. Seeing him, she waved.

Kern said to her brother, "If Bull Shannon should ask you, Jack, he whipped me last night. You stepped in to help me."

Jack Steele stared at him thoughtfully. "Must be a reason for that," he stated.

"Shannon is now a Rocky Mountain man," Kern told him, "and he'll make a good one."

"I see," Steele grinned. "I'll remember it, Kern,

but for a winner, Bull Shannon was the most badly whipped man I've ever seen."

Kern looked at the wagons lined up inside the yard. He said, "You rolling freight, Jack?"

"Up to Medicine Grove," Steele told him. "We have a load of mining machinery for Ed Morton of Consolidated Mining Company. Eighteen wagons going up. I'm taking this outfit myself."

"How did Bovard let that order get away from him?" Kern smiled.

"He was after it," Steele said, the smile leaving his face. "Even underbid me on the contract, but Norton needs this equipment in a hurry. I guaranteed I'd get it to him in two weeks or less. Ed knows me. He doesn't know Trace Bovard, so I got the order."

"So Bovard underbid you," Kern murmured. "That's the way he's going to work."

"He's been working that way all summer," Jack Steele scowled. "He's already put Pioneer and Benton Freighting out of business by taking orders away from them with those tactics."

"In this town," Kern said tersely, "we've been charging a dollar a hundred per one hundred miles for the last five years."

"Bovard's man offered Ed Norton eighty cents a hundred," Steele told him. "He might go even lower the next time."

"Any way to stop him?" Kern asked.

Jack Steele shrugged. "If he wants to haul for

nothing, Kern," he said, "who can stop him? He has the money behind him. The rest of us don't." He laughed briefly. "Reckon he's pretty sore about this Consolidated contract I took from him."

"He might try to get back at you," Kern warned him. "I'd be careful, Jack. Keep a close guard on these wagons."

"We'll roll at dawn tomorrow," Steele said. "I'll put a guard in the yard tonight."

Jennifer came up, nodding to Kern. She said, "You don't look too bad after last night."

"I was mussed up," Kern told her.

Jack Steele looked at his sister curiously, and there was a hint of humor in his blue eyes. Kern knew what he was thinking. They'd got along like cats and dogs since childhood, and now she was going out riding with him.

Jennifer said quietly, "I'm taking Kern out to the cemetery. He wants to see Uncle Billy's grave."

"I see." Jack nodded gravely. He watched them ride off a few minutes later.

Kern said to the girl, "Jack tells me you're having troubles with Ajax Overland, too."

"We'll all have plenty of trouble," Jennifer said, "before we're through."

They were going past the Sherman Hotel when Daphne Paxton came out, shimmering in white, a dazzling picture in the bright morning sunshine. Kern slowed down and tipped his hat.

"Mr. Harlan," Daphne beamed. She came over to the edge of the walk. She wore white gloves and a white hat trimmed with blue to match the color of her eyes. Standing there, she put Kern in mind of a fragile china doll that had to be handled very carefully. The broad rim of her hat protected her face from the sun. She had a creamy complexion, in marked contrast to Jennifer Steele's sun-browned face.

"How are you feeling," Kern asked her, "after your experience of yesterday?"

"It was dreadful," Daphne murmured. She closed her eyes for a moment. "I'm so thankful you came along, Mr. Harlan." She glanced over at Jennifer then, and Kern said:

"Miss Paxton, Miss Steele."

"How do you do?" Jennifer said rather stiffly. She was wearing the usual worn Levi's and a clean blue flannel shirt this morning. Her black hair was pushed in under the flat-crowned hat she wore, and Kern doubted if she'd spent too much time with it that morning.

"You are Mr. Jack Steele's sister?" Daphne asked, and her eyes moved from Jennifer's worn boots to her hat.

"I am Jack Steele's sister," Jennifer nodded, and there was a glint in her hazel eyes.

"I met your brother," Daphne murmured. "A very fine gentleman."

"All gentlemen are very fine," Jennifer observed rather coldly.

"Of course," Daphne laughed, and she looked at Kern again. She said, "I shall not keep you from your ride, Mr. Kern. Have a pleasant time."

"We're going out to Uncle Billy's grave," Kern explained. "I haven't been there yet."

"I'm so sorry," Daphne murmured.

They rode off then, Jennifer staring straight ahead of her, lips tight, saying nothing. Then she mimicked bitterly, "I'm *so* thankful you came along, Mr. Harlan."

"She was in trouble," Kern scowled.

"Out of her own stupidity," Jennifer snapped. "She shouldn't have been out riding alone. What happened out there, anyway?"

"A couple of Delawares tried to steal her horse," Kern said.

"And you came to the rescue." Jennifer smiled disdainfully. "If she'd been carrying a gun or rifle the way she should have, those Delawares wouldn't have come within a mile of her."

"Eastern women don't carry guns," Kern scowled, and he was thinking that this was the way it always had been between them. They'd never got along. For one reason or another they were always quarreling.

"Eastern women," Jennifer Steele said thinly, "carry plenty of other weapons besides guns."

"All right," Kern growled. "Forget about it."

They moved up the slope toward the cemetery a mile or so out of town, and Kern said, "So Ajax is underbidding the other outfits in this town. Jack tells me Bovard has forced Pioneer and Benton Freighting out of business with those tactics."

"He'll break more of them, too," Jennifer said slowly. "We're all glad you're back in town, Kern, to take over Rocky Mountain. Your outfit is the oldest in the business, and the most respected. The other freight lines look to you to fight Ajax. Jack told me that the other day. If Ajax can break you, most of the others will give up too."

Kern frowned. It was a logical conclusion Jennifer was drawing. Rocky Mountain Freighting, the first freight line in Nebraska City, had a high reputation on the frontier. If a well-established line like that gave up the fight, the others might figure it was no use for them to try to fight either, and sell out to Ajax. In a very short while, then, Trace Bovard would control the overland freighting industry, and with it the destinies of literally thousands of people.

"Rocky Mountain," Kern said quietly, "has been in business since 1851. We intend to stay in business. It was Rocky Mountain wagons that kept the frontier alive during the big war back East when the Indians were moving in closer all the time. I hope to have Rocky Mountain wagons on the trail right up until the railroad gets here and pushes out into the Northwest."

"We all hope you do," Jennifer said.

They had reached the little picket fence surrounding the cemetery, and both of them dismounted without a word. Kern followed Jennifer in through the gate and down past rows of headboards, the writing on many of them already indistinct, weathering in the hot plains sun.

At the far end of the cemetery, Jennifer stopped at a fresh mound on which the grass was just beginning to grow again. A new headboard had been set up, and there were fresh flowers in a bottle in front of the headboard.

Kern took off his hat. He stood there for some moments in silence, and then he said, "Who brought the flowers?"

Jennifer hesitated before answering. "I did," she said. "Uncle Billy was almost like a father to me, too. I—I didn't know my own father very well when he died."

Kern nodded. His strong fingers turning the hat around and around, he looked toward the west. He could see the trailer of dust in the sky, and the white-topped wagons beneath the dust, moving toward Nebraska City—his outfit, Everett Green leading them, his wagons, which once had been Billy McCloud's.

"He was a good man," Jennifer Steele said. "None of us would like to see his company fold up."

"It won't fold up," Kern promised. He was

still looking off into the distance, watching his wagons coming in.

They rode out then, and thirty minutes later joined up with Green's slowly moving outfit. The lank commissary had a pipe in his mouth as he rode along at the head of the column. He said when Kern came up:

"We still in business, or did Ajax Overland root us out?"

"We're in business," Kern smiled.

"And you had your little fight with Bull Shannon," Green murmured. "I can see the marks of his fists on your face. How are you, Miss Steele?"

"Very well," Jennifer smiled.

"Any trouble on the trail?" Kern asked him.

"No trouble with Rocky Mountain wagons on the trail," Green said meditatively. "It's in town that we have to worry, Kern. Bovard been after you yet?"

"He's offered our men more money," Kern told him.

Green nodded. "And the boys are staying with us," he said. "I could have told you that."

"I'm giving them more money," Kern said as they rode along beside the commissary.

Everett Green looked at him. He said dryly, "You don't have too much to give, Kern. Be careful."

"We'll get more contracts," Kern said. "We're

going to keep these wagons going right up until the first snow, and even after that."

Everett Green glanced over at Jennifer Steele. He said jocularly, "Rival freighting representative with us, Kern, but do you have any prospects?"

"Figured on going up to Fort McLane within the next day or two," Kern murmured, "and seeing about the government hauling contract there."

"McLane?" Jennifer said quickly. "Benton Freighting has had that contract for years."

"Benton Freighting's out of business," Kern observed.

"Ajax Overland gobbled them up," Jennifer said, "which means that they take over all Benton contracts, too."

"They have to?" Kern asked her quietly.

Jennifer grimaced a little. "If you go after that contract," she said, "you'll be bucking Trace Bovard directly."

"About time," Kern murmured, "that somebody bucked him directly, isn't it?"

"We'll be needing contracts like that," Everett Green said, "if you're increasing the pay of the teamsters and yardmen."

"We're going after everything," Kern told him. "We can't underbid Ajax Overland, but we can beat their time on the road on any shipment we take out, and that'll make the difference. Most of these contractors will pay more money if they can get their supplies and mining machinery a week sooner than they expected."

"Jack is talking the same way," Jennifer nodded approvingly. "Ajax will be working with inexperienced men and animals. If we can show the shippers that Ajax wagons are the slowest on the trail, we might have them."

Everett Green smiled wryly. "You don't figure Trace Bovard will sit back and let you beat him to the draw?" he asked. "I'd watch that hombre all day long, and most of the night, too."

"We'll watch him," Kern said tersely. "There's much more than just Rocky Mountain Freighting involved here."

They rolled into town a half hour later, the big oxen hauling the wagons down the main street, turning in at the Rocky Mountain yards. As they went past the Ajax Overland yard, Kern saw Trace Bovard near the cattle corral, watching some of his teamsters break in pairs of oxen.

Bovard turned to watch the Rocky Mountain wagons go by. He was smoking one of his Mexican cigarillos, and he stood there, his hands in his back pockets, a solid man, hat pulled forward over his eyes, the smoke lifting from the cigarillo in his mouth.

Bull Shannon was in the Rocky Mountain yard when Kern came in with the outfit. The Bull nodded. He said a little gruffly, "Ready to work this mornin', Harlan."

"Good," Kern said. "We'll have an outfit made up in a few days. I want you to take a dozen wagons up to Madison Point along the river. It'll be a ten-day journey there and back. You'll have complete charge of the outfit, Bull."

Bull Shannon stared at him. "Never handled an outfit in my life," he muttered. "I'm a teamster, Harlan."

"From now on," Kern smiled, "you're one of my wagonmasters, Bull. You've had plenty of experience along the trail, and you're a fighter. We're going to need fighters to handle these wagons."

Everett Green spat and said softly, "Very true, my friend."

"You'll make up the crew and cargo for Shannon, Mr. Green," Kern told him. "Fifty ton of wheat in bags on the wharf. Steamer can't go upriver because of low water. That wheat is needed at the new Army post being built at the Point."

Burton Reeves had come out of the office to look at the wagons, and he was standing nearby as Kern spoke. The office superintendent said now, "Bad business sending an inexperienced man on a trip like that, Harlan. I figured you'd be taking those wagons yourself."

Kern shook his head. "I'm going up to Fort McLane," he stated.

Reeves lifted his eyebrows. "Fort McLane?"

he repeated. "We've never taken a cargo up there before."

"We're after the old Benton Freighting contract up to the post," Kern explained. "I'm going up to see the commanding officer at McLane. I think I can convince him that Rocky Mountain Freighting can beat the best time Ajax Overland can make by six to eight days on any haul."

Reeves rubbed his thin hands together. He said, "I thought all Benton contracts went over to Ajax Overland when Ajax bought them out."

"This one," Kern smiled, "we're going after. I should be up at McLane in four or five days." He turned to Jennifer, who was standing nearby, and he said, "I'll ride over to your yard with you. I want to see Jack before he leaves tomorrow morning."

Jennifer nodded. "He's making up cargo now," she said. "You might find him down at the wharf."

They rode that way, moving past a score of river steamers tied up along the river. Jack Steele's wagons were drawn up near the side-wheeler *James Madison*. Heavy mining machinery was being loaded on the wagons under the watchful eye of Jack Steele.

The big blond-haired man waved in greeting as they came up. He grinned at his sister, and Kern saw the affection come into her eyes. He remembered how close these two were. Jack

Steele had raised his sister from childhood after their parents passed away. He'd been father and mother as well as big brother to her.

Jennifer said, "How's it coming?"

"We should be loaded by late afternoon," Jack told her. "I'll get a few hours' sleep tonight, and we'll roll before dawn." He looked at Kern and he said, "You back in business, Kern, or still taking it easy after your trip in from Denver?"

"Kern is going up to Fort McLane after that Benton hauling contract," Jennifer said.

Steele stared at Kern thoughtfully. "You're really bucking the tiger," he chuckled. "Bovard hasn't showed his claws yet, but I've an idea he can be tough."

"I can be tough, too," Kern observed.

Jennifer said, "You be careful on this trip, Jack."

The brother laughed. "Been careful all my life," he grinned. "Anything I can do for you up at Medicine Grove, Kern?" he asked.

Kern shook his head. "Get your load through," he said. "That's a big enough job."

He shook hands with the big man, and he nodded to Jennifer, thanking her for taking him out to the grave. As he rode away from the wharf he glanced back over his shoulder, and he saw Jack Steele and Jennifer in earnest consultation. He had the queer feeling that something was going to happen very shortly. He'd had that same feeling when he rode away from Nebraska City months before after saying good-by to Uncle Billy. He'd come back to Billy McCloud's grave.

In the early hours of the morning he heard Jack Steele's wagons moving through the streets of Nebraska City, the creak of yokes, the rumble of the big wheels, and the hoarse cries of the bullwhackers as they snapped their whips. As he lay there on his bed, fully awake, that feeling came back to him. He didn't sleep well the remainder of the night.

Chapter Six

At seven o'clock in the morning Kern rode out of Nebraska City. Fort McLane, an Army post on the forks of the Broken Bow and Bear Rivers, was a five-day journey by horseback to the northwest. With the cool morning breeze blowing in his face, his pack horse trailing behind him, he left the bull trail a few miles out of town and struck up into the hills, where he could avoid the dust below.

The horse he rode was a big bay gelding, one of the best animals in his corrals. Moving at a fairly brisk pace through the morning hours, he paused for a rest at Smith Creek, where the freighting trail from the north swung down to run eventually into the Fort McLane trail. Far to the north he could see the dust banner of Jack Steele's wagons in the brassy sky. He watched that trailer of dust for some minutes in silence as his horses drank from the creek, and then he was off again, paralleling the McLane trail, passing another freight outfit that was on the way in to Nebraska City.

He camped that night at Beaver Springs, and the following night at tiny Fort Hill, a former Army post but now a trading center and a supply depot along the trail. Fort Hill was on the Platte, and in the morning he walked the bay across the shallow, half-mile-wide river, pushing out into the low hills beyond.

Buffalo grazed on the slopes here, vast herds of them, stretching almost to the horizon, and he had to swing around to the east to get around them. He dropped a young cow that evening, and he had fresh meat at his night camp.

At three o'clock in the afternoon of the fifth day he rode into Fort McLane. He hadn't been up to the post in nearly two years, and the change in the place amazed him. McLane had not been much larger than Fort Hill at that time, but it dwarfed the smaller post now.

A heavy log stockade had been erected. The rows of barracks along the stockade walls could accommodate three to four hundred men. A huge parade ground had been set out in the center of the fort, and high up on top of the pine flagpole the flag rippled in the breeze coming off the river.

Loosing his horses in the post stockade, Kern made his way directly toward headquarters, a two-story log structure facing on the parade grounds. He was moving past Officers' Row when he heard a sharp cry from the veranda of one of the buildings.

A tall, brown-haired man wearing a captain's bars strode toward him, grinning, hand outstretched. The officer called, "Kern! Kern Harlan!"

Kern pulled up, recognizing the man immediately. He'd met Captain Randolph Manning at Fort Logan far to the south when making hauls there, and they'd become very friendly. On a number of occasions they'd gone hunting together, and once they'd got into a brush with a band of Kiowas.

They shook hands warmly, and Randolph Manning said, "What brings you up this way, Kern?"

"After hauling contracts," Kern smiled. "I might ask the same thing of you. Figured you were pretty well set at Logan."

"No man is set in the Army," Manning grinned. "I was transferred two months ago. They're building up McLane as an advance post to protect the emigrant wagons that are starting to pour through this way."

Kern nodded. "Colonel Howlett still in command here?" he asked.

"Still here." Captain Manning took him by the arm and steered him toward headquarters. He said cheerily, "I'll put in a good word for you and for Rocky Mountain Freighting. You shouldn't have any trouble getting the contract."

Kern smiled a little, much pleased with the way the affair was turning out. He sat across the desk from Colonel Howlett, commanding officer at McLane, a few minutes later, listening to Captain Manning talk.

"Mr. Harlan," Manning said, "is rated the best wagonmaster in the business. His Rocky

Mountain wagons have broken trail records on practically every route out of Nebraska City. I've known him for several years, sir, and I can vouch for him."

Colonel Howlett, a spare, gray-haired man with a beard, rubbed his hands together thoughtfully. He had pale blue eyes with an old saber cut over the left one. He said, "Benton Freighting, the company doing most of our hauling, has been taken over by Ajax Overland. It is customary, I suppose, for us to do business with Ajax, but it is not mandatory. We are interested in speed in getting supplies here, Mr. Harlan. This post has been tripled in size during the last three months, and it will grow larger. An Army post on the western frontier needs a life line to the Missouri River and the supply steamers. In the past we have had numerous delays on our shipments from Nebraska City, and we have not been too well pleased."

Kern nodded. He said briefly, "Rocky Mountain wagons usually get through on time. Any hauls to be made up to Fort McLane I will handle personally."

"What is the fastest time you can make from Nebraska City to McLane?" Colonel Howlett asked him.

Kern thought for a moment. He knew that Benton Freighting took at least three weeks to make the haul. He knew the trail; he knew his men and his stock. He said, "Fifteen days."

Colonel Howlett pursed his lips. "Our winter supply is coming up the Missouri now," he stated, "aboard the steamer *Robert Grimes*. She should dock at Nebraska City by mid-September. If you can bring that cargo up here in fifteen days from the time of loading, the McLane hauling contract is yours, and I can assure you that in the future it will be a large one—possibly the largest in the West."

Kern Harlan's eyes flicked. "I think we can do it," he said promptly, and he stood up, knowing that the talk was over.

"Our quartermaster will make out your assignment," Colonel Howlett smiled. "Good luck, Mr. Harlan. We'd like to do business with you."

Kern shook hands with him and went out into the sunshine with Captain Manning. He said, "I appreciate your recommendation, Captain."

Manning waved a hand. "Purely good business," he grinned. "We have to keep the men contented at the post, and when they're forced on a diet of salt pork for days at a time because the freighting wagons are held up, they don't like it. An army fights on its stomach."

"There won't be any delays with Rocky Mountain wagons," Kern told him.

They went over to the quartermaster's shed and he received his assignment in writing to pick up the Fort McLane cargo at Nebraska City.

Randolph Manning said hopefully when they came out, "I heard there were some elk up along Wine Creek, a few miles from here, Kern. Done much hunting lately?"

Kern smiled and shook his head. "We'll have to save that until my next trip up here. I've got to get back."

"It's a date," Manning nodded.

At Captain Manning's invitation, Kern ate at the single officers' table that night, and he was sitting on the veranda at dusk when the two hot, dusty riders came through the post gates. They passed by along the edge of the parade grounds, and Kern spotted the brands on the hips of the horses. They were both "A.O." The Ajax Overland representatives had arrived to sign the hauling contract at Fort McLane.

Kern smiled faintly as they rode by. He saw them going up to headquarters a half hour later, and then he watched them come out and walk glumly toward the sutler's store for a drink. He walked down that way himself later in the evening after Captain Manning had to excuse himself in order to make up a report.

The two Ajax men stood at the little bar, the corners of their mouths down as they drank. He didn't know either of them personally, and this was not surprising, because Trace Bovard had been bringing in entirely new personnel.

One man was short and shifty-eyed, in a long,

black frock coat. He had a wolfish face with big spaces between his teeth. The second man was taller, with bleary blue eyes and a scraggly horse-tail mustache. He looked at Kern sourly as he came in. They were both drinking steadily, silently, engaged in their own thoughts.

At the food counter Kern ordered a small package of coffee for the return trip, along with some dried apples. The sutler, who knew him, said:

"Leaving in the morning, Mr. Harlan?"

Kern paid for his purchases. "Aim to," he said. He noticed that the two men at the bar turned around to stare at him. He watched the sutler wrap up the packages, and he was turning to go when the tall man with the mustache said to him:

"You Kern Harlan of Rocky Mountain Freighting?"

"That's right," Kern said.

The Ajax man stared at him coldly, the liquor glass in his hand. He said tersely, "You kind o' stole a march on us up here, Harlan, didn't you?"

Kern smiled at him. He said, "If your wagons travel as fast as you do over the trail, you'll never be able to get or hold another hauling contract."

The man with the mustache said softly, "When you buck Ajax, mister, you're walkin' right into a nest o' hornets."

"That right?" Kern smiled. He just stood there, smiling at the two Ajax men, letting them make what they wanted to out of it, not caring.

They saw this in his face, too, and they were a little wary. He had a gun on his hip, and from the way he carried it, he knew how to use it.

The short man with the shifty eyes said grimly, "Our outfit took over Benton Freighting, mister, an' that means we take their contracts, too."

"Tell that to Colonel Howlett," Kern advised him. "He handles the post business. I'm only a freight man."

"Reckon you won't be in the freight business too long, Harlan," the tall man murmured, "if you try to cut in on us like this."

Kern's gray eyes seemed to change color. He took a step forward, and he said gently, "I aim to be in the freight business long after the Ajax wagons have disappeared from the trail. You can tell that to Trace Bovard."

Neither man said anything. They stood there at the bar, the shifty-eyed man licking his lips nervously and the tall man twisting the liquor glass around and around in his hand.

Kern went out into the night. He left McLane at dawn while it was still cool, intending if possible to return to Nebraska City in four days instead of five. With this Fort McLane contract practically assured, he had much other business to do. He needed more stock in the yards now; before the winter came he'd have to go down to St. Louis to order a few more wagons for the trade. Then there was Daphne Paxton. He would like to see her when he returned. He'd been thinking much of her these long days in the saddle.

The first night he camped at Little Springs off the ox trail, and the second night out he camped about thirty miles north of the Platte, on the edge of the great buffalo herd. He shot another cow that night, roasting one of the steaks over a small fire he'd built down in a hollow.

Where the great herd was there were usually Indians. The Cheyennes, who hunted these grounds, were friendly enough, but there was always the possibility of running into war parties, or even hunting parties from other tribes, and a lone white man with two good horses on the trail was always in danger of losing not only his horses, but his hair.

He tied the bay and the pack animal in a thicket close by, and then rolled into his blanket, using the saddle as a pillow. The night was clear and cool after the sun went down. Off in the distance he could hear the roar of young buffalo bulls as they challenged each other. He was safe enough where he was, because the big herd would not drift very much during the night, and he expected to be off again before dawn.

When he fell asleep, he could still hear the distant roar of the bulls. When he awoke it was still night. The positions of the stars had changed, but they were still very bright in the dark vault of the sky. He thought at first that it was the roaring of the bulls that had awakened him, and he lay in his blanket, listening.

There was a sound, but it was different. He'd heard that sound once before when he'd seen a big band of buffalo stampede during a violent electric storm. The ground was vibrating beneath him, and he sat up hurriedly, casting aside the blanket.

The sound was coming closer. It seemed to be just beyond the lip of the hollow. And then he heard something else—high-pitched yells in the distance beyond the hammer of hundreds of hoofs.

In the thicket where he'd tied the bay and the pack horse he heard frightened whinnying. They, too, had sensed what was coming, and they were struggling frantically to tear loose from the tether ropes.

Leaping to his feet, Kern snatched up his gun belt, which he'd placed at his side. He sprinted for the thicket just as the first scattered buffalo loomed up over the lip of the hollow. They tumbled down, several of them losing their footing, rolling end over end down into the hollow. One of them landed in the nearly dead fire, scattering hot ashes, snorting in fear as it scrambled to its feet.

The pack horse had broken loose from its rope and was scrambling up out of the hollow. Kern reached the big bay just as the animal snapped its rope. A heavy, shaggy creature shot past him as he leaped for the bare back of the bay. Others were all around him, surging past blindly, snorting, puffing, a musky smell to them.

His gun belt dangling from his hand, gripping the mane of the big bay, Kern let the gelding run. He gripped the flanks of the animal with his knees as they came up out of the hollow, buffalo all around him now, pounding toward the south. He had nothing to worry about as long as the big bay didn't step into a hole and go down. The gelding was moving along smoothly, rapidly drawing up to the lead buffalo in this stampede.

Behind him the animals were still coming, but he didn't hear those high-pitched human yells any more. There had been no gunfire, and that could mean an Indian hunt, if Indians hunted at night. Kern Harlan knew that they didn't—not ever. Those yells, then, had come from the lips of white men—men who had deliberately started this stampede of a small portion of the big herd, and run them over the hollow in which he'd made his night camp.

When he'd pulled the bay out of the path of the herd, he slowed down, buckled on the gun belt, and sat there, listening to the heavy puffing of the horse and the distant rumble of the hoofs. He'd lost his pack horse and his supplies; he'd lost his saddle and his blankets; but he was alive, and men had definitely tried to kill him tonight.

For one brief moment he was tempted to turn around and ride back, to search for the cowardly crew that had stampeded the buffalo on him. Without a saddle, and without supplies, it was foolish to linger here. He was fairly certain, though, who had been behind the murder attempt, and he was fairly certain, too, that he wasn't going to forget them.

He shot another cow at the edge of the herd at dawn, cut out the tongue, and roasted some of it over a small fire. He grinned at the thought of riding all the way back to Nebraska City without a saddle, but he was saved from this ordeal in the late afternoon when he came up with a Great Western Freighting outfit swinging down from Camp Adams on the Cheyenne, headed for Nebraska City. He was able to borrow a saddle and blankets from the wagonmaster in charge, a man by the name of Barclay.

Barclay said to him, laughingly, "Injuns jump you, Kern?"

"White Indians," Kern said tersely. "They tried to run a buffalo herd over me."

Barclay spat and then whistled softly. "Things gettin' pretty rough on the trail," he murmured. "Know who they were, Kern?"

"I know," Kern nodded.

He moved away from the bull outfit, riding

till nearly midnight that night before making his camp.

He came into Nebraska City at noon the fourth day, pushing on steadily after crossing the Platte. As he rode into his own yard he noticed that a crowd was gathering down under the arch of the Steele Freighting yard.

Tom Moran came over to take his horse. He looked at Kern closely, and then he said, "Reckon you ran into a little trouble, too, Kern. That ain't your saddle."

"What's going on over at the Steele yard?" Kern asked him. He stood there, just inside the arch, looking down the street.

Moran moistened his lips. "You ain't heard," he said grimly. "Reckon you're the only one in town ain't heard, Kern. They're bringin' Jack Steele in."

Kern felt a cold chill go through him. "Bringing him in?" he repeated.

Moran nodded. "Trail pirates shot up Jack's outfit up at Willow Creek three days ago," he said. "Jack ain't rollin' any more freight, Kern."

Chapter Seven

She was sitting in a chair in Jack Steele's little cubbyhole of an office. She sat by the window, looking out across the sun-baked yard. The crowd that had been gathered there an hour ago had dispersed. They could hear the heavy beat of the blacksmith's hammer, and Kern saw the sparks showering up inside the smithy door. Two men were jacking up a wagon, and a third man stood by, watching them, wiping his face with a red handkerchief.

Kern said, "Who did it?"

Jennifer Steele shook her head. She just sat there, looking out the window. She had not cried, and Kern Harlan found himself wishing that she would. She had not even cried when they'd brought her the news the day before. Everett Green had told him that. He'd had the unpleasant duty of breaking the news to her, because a Rocky Mountain crew had come across Steele's burning wagons and ambushed crew. A rider had been sent back to Nebraska City with the news.

Kern shook his head. "They were white men," he said. "Border ruffians, half-breeds, the scum of the frontier saloons, renegade Indians driven out of their tribes."

He'd heard that there were about fifty in

the band that had suddenly swooped down on Steele's small outfit. They'd worn mostly white men's clothing, but their faces had been painted for concealment. Five other Steele teamsters had been killed, and every wagon burned.

Kern said uncomfortably, "You have any plans for the future, Jennifer?" He didn't know this girl any more. There was ice in her heart. He had the feeling that he would have liked to put his arms around her and comfort her, but she held him away by her coldness. She didn't want comfort. She just sat there, staring out the window, no expression on her face. She knew who had killed her brother. Kern knew it, too.

Jennifer said abruptly, "How would you like to buy out Steele Freighting, Kern?"

The question caught Kern by surprise. He'd expected her to continue with the business. She knew it as well as Jack Steele did. She had a few pretty good wagonmasters with the company, and she could handle a trail outfit as well as any of them if she wished.

Kern said slowly, "You—you selling out?"

"I'm selling out," Jennifer nodded. "I'd rather see you get the business than Ajax."

He felt a vague sense of disappointment in her. She was a fighter, but she wasn't going to fight. She was giving up, leaving the freighting business that her dead brother had built up through the years.

"Reckon we can make a deal," Kern said. "You leaving Nebraska City?"

Jennifer shook her head. "I don't know yet," she said. She wasn't even looking at him. She still looked out across the yard.

"Better think things over a few days," Kern advised. "Don't jump yet until you know where you're jumping."

"I'll bring Jason Dow over to your office tomorrow afternoon," Jennifer said, "after the funeral. We'll let him put a value on the property."

Her voice was steady, unemotional, even when she mentioned the funeral. She wasn't going to cry, not even tomorrow. Kern knew that now.

He got up. He said awkwardly, "Anything I can do, Jennifer, let me know."

Jennifer Steele nodded. When he went out, she was still sitting there, looking out the window.

He went back to his own yard and into the office. He said to Reeves, who was sitting at his desk, "We have the McLane contract if we can bring their first cargo out to the post in fifteen days. That's the deal I made with Colonel Howlett."

Reeves rubbed his ink-stained hands. "Pretty fast time," he observed. He looked over his fingertips at the ledger on the desk in front of him. Then he said, "An Ajax man inside to see you, Mr. Harlan. Just came in." He nodded toward Kern's office.

Kern's eyes hardened. "Bovard?" he asked.

"Ajax attorney," Reeves stated. "Man by the name of Dillingworth. New man in town."

Kern nodded. "Another thing," he said casually. "Rocky Mountain is buying out Steele Freighting. Miss Steele is leaving the business."

He saw the surprise start up in Reeves' slate-colored eyes. The office superintendent put both hands flat on the book in front of him.

"Steele Freighting selling out?" he repeated.

"We close the deal tomorrow afternoon," Kern told him, and then he walked on into his own office.

Dillingworth was sitting primly in a chair near Kern's desk, a small, spare, bespectacled man with a bald head. He had a long, pointed nose, putting Kern in mind of a crane. His eyes were weak and watery behind the glasses, and he had a nasal voice that Kern found distasteful immediately.

The Ajax lawyer said briskly, "Heard you were back in town, Mr. Harlan. I represent Ajax Overland Freighting." He handed Kern his card and Kern looked at it. It read, "J. P. Dillingworth, Attorney at Law."

Sitting down behind his desk, Kern said, "What's your business, Mr. Dillingworth?"

J. P. Dillingworth wasted no time. He said pompously, "Mr. Harlan, Ajax Overland would like to know your top price for Rocky Mountain

Freighting. We are in a position to buy you out—at a reasonable price, of course."

Kern leaned back in the chair. He took a cigar from the box on the table, bit off the end, and then lighted it. He said softly, "So Ajax is in a position to buy me out."

"We are prepared," J. P. Dillingworth went on sonorously, consulting a sheath of papers he'd taken out of his brief case, "to pay you a fair and equitable price for your establishment, Mr. Harlan. Mr. Bovard has authorized me to name that price."

"What is it?" Kern asked curiously.

"Fifteen thousand dollars," the lawyer stated. "You will be able to retire and live in luxury, Mr. Harlan. I consider you indeed fortunate."

"You do?" Kern smiled. He knew beyond any shadow of doubt that Rocky Mountain Freighting was worth at least double the price Bovard was ready to pay.

Dillingworth looked at him curiously as if a little surprised at the mildness of Kern's reaction. He said, "We are aware of Rocky Mountain's financial status, Mr. Harlan. You lost money last year and the year before. Business is not good. You should consider yourself fortunate that Mr. Bovard has made so generous an offer."

Kern puffed on the cigar for a few moments in silence as if deliberating on the offer. He stared at the desk, at the ink bottle and pens. He said, "You have anything more to say, Mr. Dillingworth?"

The lawyer blinked. "No. That is all. That is our final offer, sir."

"Get out," Kern told him. His voice was flat, sharp, but not loud.

J. P. Dillingworth stared at him. "Sir?"

"Get out," Kern said softly. "You hear me, mister?" He got up and came around the table.

The red came into the little lawyer's face. He bristled like a bantam rooster, and he snapped, "I am not accustomed to being spoken to like this, Mr. Harlan. Back East, where I was engaged in business, I was considered—"

He never finished the sentence. Kern picked up the ink bottle, held it over the little man's bald pate, and let the black ink pour out across his skull, emptying the bottle completely.

Dillingworth gasped and leaped back, upsetting the chair. He was spluttering, the ink streaming down his face, giving him a ludicrous appearance.

Walking toward the door, Kern called back over his shoulder, "Next time tell Bovard to come himself." He went out.

In the yard he met Everett Green coming out of the tool shed, and he said, "We're buying Steele Freighting tomorrow, Everett. Jennifer is selling out."

Green stared at him. "Didn't expect that," he admitted. "Didn't figure she was the type would run away. I thought she'd fight Bovard from here to hell and back again until the day she died."

Kern looked across the yard. "We don't know that it was Bovard," he pointed out.

The commissary smiled. "We didn't see Bovard shoot Jack Steele down," he admitted, "but we know who it was. We know Ajax didn't like it because Steele stood up against them." He looked at Kern thoughtfully, and then he said, "Heard you had a little trouble on the way back from McLane."

"Not too bad," Kern murmured. "Not as bad as Jack Steele's trouble." He still had Jennifer Steele in his mind, that peculiar expression on her face as she'd sat by the window, looking out. He was even thinking about her that night as he sat opposite Daphne Paxton in the hotel dining room.

Meeting Tobias Paxton on the street that afternoon, he'd been invited to dine with them, and he'd accepted the invitation. Now Daphne said to him, poutingly, "You are very quiet tonight, Mr. Harlan."

"Mr. Harlan," the Colonel smiled, "has had a long and I trust successful journey. He is tired, my dear."

"It was successful," Kern admitted, "and nearly fatal, too."

He told them about the buffalo stampede, and Daphne stared at him, horrified.

"How terrible!" she gasped when he'd finished.

"It ended up all right," Kern scowled, "but it was a lucky thing for me that my riding horse hadn't broken his tether line a few seconds earlier."

"Buffalo stampede," Tobias Paxton murmured. "Do the buffalo run like that often, Mr. Harlan?"

"Not often," Kern said grimly. "At night they have to be disturbed a little." He hadn't told them about the shouts he'd heard behind the oncoming herd, the real reason for the stampede.

He and Colonel Paxton smoked cigars when they'd finished eating, and for the first time tonight Kern started to take notice of Daphne. She was dressed in blue, the color of her eyes, and her eyes were wide and beautiful as she watched him across the table.

When there was a lull in the conversation the Colonel suddenly hailed an acquaintance across the room, stood up, and bowed to Harlan. He said smilingly, "I trust you young people do not mind if I leave you. I remember when I was younger."

Kern reddened a little. He nodded and puffed on his cigar as Tobias Paxton moved away from the table.

Daphne smiled at him. She said softly, "I'm glad you escaped from that buffalo stampede, Kern."

"Kind of glad, myself," Kern smiled. He leaned back in the chair and said, "How are you enjoying your stay in Nebraska City?"

"It's wonderful!" Daphne laughed gaily. "I think Uncle Tobias likes it, too. He's made a great many acquaintances in town."

Kern nodded. He said curiously, "What does he intend to do here? Has he made any plans yet?"

Daphne shook her head. "I believe Uncle wants to go into business," she said. "I know he has some money to invest, but he hasn't quite decided what to do with it."

"I see," Kern murmured. The thought suddenly came to him that Uncle Tobias could profitably invest his money in Rocky Mountain Freighting. He didn't like to make this suggestion, but he certainly could use a loan, especially now that he'd committed himself to buying out the Steele line from Jennifer.

"I believe," Daphne was saying, "that we shall settle down in Nebraska City." She looked at him rather archly.

"That's good news," Kern stated. His eyes moved toward the dining-room door. Trace Bovard was coming in, making his way toward an empty table. The owner of Ajax Overland smoked the usual slim brown cigarillo. He was with another man whom Kern did not know.

Bovard spotted him, stared at him for a moment, and then said something to his companion and walked directly toward them.

Kern looked at him steadily as he came up. He nodded, but he didn't say anything. Bovard said flatly, "With your permission, Miss Paxton, I'd like a few words with Mr. Harlan."

Fright came into Daphne's blue eyes. She nodded.

Bovard turned to Kern. He said stiffly, "Mr. Harlan, I didn't particularly like your treatment of my attorney."

Kern shrugged. He looked at his cigar, and then he said, "What made you think I'd sell Rocky Mountain, Mr. Bovard?"

"I make an offer for everything I like," Bovard snapped. "If you didn't want to do business, you could have refused in a gentlemanly way."

Kern smiled at him. "Reckon I didn't like your Mr. Dillingworth, Bovard. I am sorry about the ink, though." He added, thoughtfully, "It was a good bottle of ink."

He saw Daphne staring at him.

Trace Bovard said tersely, "If you intend to make trouble, Harlan, I'd like to inform you that Ajax Overland is not running away from it."

"I'm not making trouble," Kern said coldly. "I've already had it. Buffalo trouble." He watched Bovard's face closely as he said this, and he thought he saw a faint reaction deep down in the man's cool green eyes.

"You talk in riddles," Bovard growled.

"You can tell your two representatives whom I met in Fort McLane," Harlan stated grimly, "that the next time I run across them I won't talk.

I don't like coyotes who move behind a herd of buffalo."

Bovard was staring at him, lips tight. He said, "When you went after that McLane contract, Harlan, you bit off more than you can chew. That business belongs to Ajax."

"Business belongs to whoever gets it," Kern told him. "You're new in this country, Bovard. You haven't learned that yet."

"I'm learning fast," Bovard grated. Turning to Daphne Paxton then, he said, "My apologies, Miss Paxton, for this intrusion." The cigarillo tilted toward the ceiling, he strode away.

Daphne said to Kern, "I'm curious. What happened to Mr. Dillingworth?"

Kern smiled faintly. "I poured a bottle of ink over his head," he murmured. "Good ink, too."

Daphne laughed lightly, and then her eyes clouded. She said, "Uncle tells me Mr. Bovard is a rather hard businessman. I'd be careful of him if I were you."

"Aim to be," Kern said. He was pleased with her concern for him.

Before he left her that evening he made arrangements to take her riding the following Sunday afternoon. He went back to Uncle Billy's house, and old Amos Scott, the colored man, letting him in, said:

"Sound like Mr. McCloud comin' in. Always whistlin'."

Kern grinned. He was feeling good, and then he thought of Jennifer Steele, and the good spirits left him. Tomorrow afternoon he had to meet with Jennifer to negotiate for Steele Freighting. Remembering her face, he could not feel merry.

She sat in his office across the desk from him, listening as the lawyer Dow spoke. Her mind, however, seemed to be far away, and Kern doubted whether she heard all that he was saying.

The papers had been drawn up. A fair figure had been arrived at for Steele Freighting, and Kern had agreed to it. Reeves had said to him that morning that the purchase of the line would put them in a precarious financial position, but Kern had decided to go through with it anyway. Jack Steele had built up a good freighting line. He had good wagons and sound stock, and the investment would pay off if Rocky Mountain Freighting could get the business.

Dow said briskly, "We need only sign the papers now, and arrange for payment."

"I'll give Miss Steele a draft in the morning," Kern told him. He looked at Jennifer and added, "If that's agreeable to Miss Steele."

"It's agreeable," Jennifer said.

He wondered what she was going to do with the money. The total sale price of the line had come to $18,500, a sizable sum for a single girl to have.

Watching as she signed the papers, he said casually, "You made any plans for the future, Jennifer?"

"Some," Jennifer said. Her face showed nothing. It was still cold, placid, with that peculiar expression in her eyes.

"Very unfortunate, your brother's death," the lawyer Dow said.

"Very unfortunate," Jennifer Steele agreed. She looked out the window.

When she'd gone out a few minutes later, Dow said to Kern, "What's going to happen to her, Mr. Harlan? That girl has changed."

Kern shook his head dubiously. He'd liked the other Jennifer Steele better—the girl who was constantly quarreling with him, disagreeing with him. This new Jennifer Steele he did not know, and he was a little afraid of her.

Standing by the window that faced on the street, he watched her striding back toward her own office, still dressed in the usual worn Levi's and faded gray flannel shirt. She walked stiffly, as if she knew exactly what she had to do and intended to do it if she died in the attempt. A cold chill went through him as he watched.

He said, "She's changed, Mr. Dow."

Then he heard Tom Moran's booming voice from the yard: "Kern—Kern Harlan!"

Running over to the other window, he put his head out. A rider had just come in, horse lathered, shaky from the tremendous effort. A crowd of Rocky Mountain yardmen was gathering around the rider, who had slipped from the saddle and was being half supported by Everett Green and Joe Bannister, the teamster. Kern saw the stain of blood on his left shoulder.

Moran called laconically, "Trouble up at Elder Creek, Kern. Trail pirates raidin' Bull Shannon's outfit."

Kern bolted for the door, snatching his gun belt from the hook on the wall as he raced by. He was strapping it on, coming out into the yard, when Everett Green met him.

Green said tersely, "Shannon's got his wagons corraled. He's fighting them off."

"Round up every man in the yard," Kern yelled at Moran. He raced for the stables, Green running with him, and he said, "Shannon's a fighter. He'll hold them off if anyone can."

"Ought to reach Elder Creek before night," Green said. "They're getting pretty rough in this town, Kern."

"I'll be rough, myself," Kern panted, "when we get back."

He saddled the big bay and led the animal out of the stable, Everett Green coming behind him, shoving a rifle in the saddle holster.

Tom Moran had lined up two dozen yardmen and teamsters. They were mounted, ready to ride. Kern led the band out under the arch over the gateway. They hammered up the main street, and he saw Daphne Paxton and her uncle sitting on the porch of the hotel as they went by. He lifted a hand to them, and he saw Tobias Paxton half rise out of his chair to watch.

As they left the town behind them, hitting into the ox trail stretching north out of Nebraska City, Everett Green said grimly, "Must be the same bunch butchered Jack Steele."

Kern nodded. He stared straight ahead as he rode, and he said grimly, "Reckon I owe them one, Everett, for Jennifer."

Elder Creek was about a dozen miles north of the city, the first night stopping place on the way out, and the last on the way in. Bull Shannon must have been approaching the creek when the band struck at him. According to the rider who had broken through the cordon, Shannon had managed to beat off the first attack and circle his wagons for a stand.

They left the trail about two miles out of town, Kern striking overland, a rougher but faster route to the creek. At the top of Dead Man's Bluff, a high ridge overlooking the Missouri a half mile away, they stopped to breathe their horses, and then they pushed on again.

One rider had to drop out when his horse slipped on the rough terrain, coming up limping. Kern waved to the rider to make his way back to town. He kept going, listening now for distant shots.

The sun had dropped down behind the row of dun-colored hills on the western horizon, but there was still plenty of light in the sky. They were within a few miles of the creek now, with the horses beginning to feel the pace.

Everett Green said slowly, "I don't hear anything, Kern. It might be that we're a little too late."

Kern's face was taut as he pushed the big bay on. He could not afford to lose those wagons and the valuable stock. After paying for the Steele line, he would need every wagon and every head of stock he possessed.

Green said, "Why in hell would trail pirates raid empty wagons, Kern? Shannon was coming back from his trip. He didn't have a return cargo, did he?"

"They're empty," Kern nodded. "This isn't a raid for loot. Somebody's trying to break us, and this is the way to do it. Burn our wagons, slaughter the stock, and murder the men, and you have no line."

"Who," Green asked, "is somebody?"

Kern didn't say anything. He rode on, shoulders hunched, and then he reached forward and loosened the flap of his saddle holster. Beyond the next ridge they would be able to see the Elder Creek camping ground.

There were no shots, no sounds except the pounding of the horses' hoofs, the creak of saddles, and the jangle of accouterments. They were going up the slope, the horses puffing, when the guns opened up from the other side of the ridge.

There was a quick spatter of rifle fire, and then wild yells. Kern thought he could hear Bull Shannon's deep-voiced roar in the background. He waved a hand and called, "Straight ahead."

The two dozen riders swept over the top of the ridge and tore down the other side. Shannon's wagons were still intact, drawn up in a rough circle, the stock inside. Puffs of smoke broke from the tops of the wagons where many of Shannon's teamsters were lying.

About forty or fifty riders were driving in from the west as Kern's men came up from the south. They were within a hundred yards of the enclosure, firing, yelling, dark shapes against the gathering dusk of the night. They were not Indians; they were not riding Indian ponies. Kern had fought off enough Indian raids to be able to differentiate between the large, bony white man's horse and the small, shaggy, spotted Indian mustang.

"Get 'em!" Kern yelled. He drove straight toward the attacking body, his teamsters following him, and then he heard the triumphant yells from the wagon corral.

The attacking band had slowed down when they saw the reinforcements coming up. Kern had the rifle out of the holster. He fired at the nearest man, knocking him from the saddle.

The Rocky Mountain men were spreading out as they came down the slope, firing steadily. Then Bull Shannon roared from the enclosure, "Give 'em hell, boys! Come on!"

The besieged teamsters scrambled down from the tops of the wagons and raced out of the enclosure, firing as they ran. The fire from two sides was too much for the trail pirates.

Kern heard one of them call sharply, "That's all! That's all!"

Everett Green, reloading his rifle beside Kern, said laconically, "Reckon that wasn't an Injun, Kern."

A half dozen of the attacking band had been dropped, and the others were turning, riding away into the shadows. Kern, in the lead of his own band, came up beside one of them, anxious to make a capture. His rifle was empty, but he swung the stock at the man's head, missing by a matter of inches.

The rider swung in his saddle, pointed his pistol directly at Kern's face, and pulled the trigger. Kern, attempting to duck down, heard the sharp click of the hammer as it fell on an empty cylinder. He caught a glimpse of the rider's face just before his bay horse stumbled in a tiny gully and he had to kick his boots free of the stirrups and leap clear.

The rider's face was painted with black and white stripes. It was a broad face with a flattened nose and high cheekbones, but the man was not an Indian. He wore a short brown jacket and a black slouch hat. His hair, from what Kern could make out, was brown and long, not Indian's hair.

Rolling as he fell, Kern came up on one knee. He'd lost the rifle, but yanking the Colt gun from the holster, he fired several shots at the fleeing riders. They were already disappearing around clumps of willows and elder bushes. He didn't think he'd hit any of them.

Everett Green slipped out of the saddle and raced over to him. He called anxiously, "You all right, Kern?"

"All right," Kern growled. "I wanted one of those chaps alive."

"Some of them hit back there," Green told him. "One of them might still have life in him."

The Rocky Mountain riders, coming in on spent horses, did not pursue the trail raiders very far. Tom Moran brought them back after they'd continued the chase about a half mile beyond the creek.

Bull Shannon's men were gathered around the raiders who'd been hit. Shannon had been wounded in the side, and his flannel shirt was soggy with blood. When Kern pointed to it, the big teamster waved a hand deprecatingly.

"Lost more blood in that fight with you, Kern," he said. "Ain't nothin'."

"You did a good job," Kern told him warmly.

"Not a wagon lost," Shannon said a little proudly. "Three o' the bulls got hit in the first charge afore we could get 'em inside."

"How about the men?" Kern wanted to know.

"Some scratches," Shannon told him. "That bunch ain't good shots."

"They shot pretty well at Jack Steele," Everett Green murmured, and Shannon looked at him and then at Kern.

"This same bunch struck at Jack's small outfit a short while ago," Kern explained briefly. "Jack Steele's dead."

Bull Shannon's lower jaw fell. He said slowly, "What in hell's happenin' on this trail, Kern?"

Everett Green answered the question for him. He said quietly, "Red war is breaking out, Bull. The freighting trails are becoming too crowded."

Tom Moran came up and said, "One o' these boys ain't dead yet, Kern. Rest of 'em are pretty well shot up."

Kern went over with him to the wounded man on the ground. He lay in the short grass, writhing, a bullet in his stomach. This man's face was also painted, but like the others, he was a white man.

Crouching down, Kern said to him quietly, "Who sent you, mister?"

"Go to hell," the man muttered.

"You're dying," Kern told him. "Don't be a fool."

The man looked up at him. They brought a flaming torch out from the enclosure so that they could see. The flickering yellow light illuminated his face, making it hideous with the painted stripes and the pain lines.

"Was it Bovard?" Kern asked.

The wounded man's lips were moving. He gasped for air, his body twisting on the ground. He looked at Kern and opened his mouth as if to say something, and then his head fell back and he was still.

Bull Shannon said sourly, "Reckon that one's no good any more, Kern. We'll have to catch you another one."

Kern stood up. He looked around at the circle of silent men, and he said tersely, "When we catch one, there's going to be hell to pay in Nebraska City."

Chapter Eight

A week after Shannon's outfit rolled into Nebraska City, every wagon intact, Kern received the news from Everett Green that a Wilson Freight outfit had been hit by the trail pirates a dozen miles north of the Platte, and then another, this time a fifteen-wagon outfit from the Wyandotte yards, burned about halfway en route to Denver.

In each instance the report indicated that the same band had made the attack—undoubtedly white men and half-breeds, painted as Indians, attacking with all the ferocity of the Plains Indians, but augmented by the white man's cunning and sagacity.

Everett Green said grimly, "They hit at the small outfits on the trail, and they hit fast and hard. It's all over in a matter of minutes. They know which outfit to hit, too, and they pick their ground for the attack, which is something the Sioux and the Kiowas never bothered about."

"Four raids in about two weeks," Kern growled. "If it keeps on like this, the smaller companies will be afraid to send an outfit on the road. Very few of us can afford large escorts, and you need a fairly large escort to hold off fifty to seventy-five cutthroats."

Green said, "Steele Freighting hit, and then Rocky Mountain. Then Wilson Freighting and the Wyandotte line. Everybody but Ajax Overland."

They sat in Kern's office, smoking cigars, looking out across the sun-baked yard. It was hot, but not with the heat now of midsummer. Already Kern could sense a change in the weather. This was early September, with the nights becoming fairly cold, and the heat of the day not the burning heat of summer.

"Ajax Overland," Kern murmured grimly, and at that moment Tom Moran stuck his head through the door.

The teamster said, "Hate like hell to break in on you, Kern."

"Go ahead," Kern said.

"News just came in," Moran said. "That trail crew just hit at one o' Bovard's outfits."

Kern's feet came off the desk and the cigar drooped in his mouth. He looked at Everett Green. Surprise was in Green's face, and then the commissary drawled, "No wagons burned, Tom?"

"None," Moran shook his head. "Didn't lose no stock, either, far as we heard. This bunch just hit at 'em eighty miles to the south near Fort Carroll. Bovard's crew drove 'em off."

Green arched his eyebrows. He said softly, "Did they, though, Tom?"

The teamster scratched his head. Kern was

smiling grimly, also, now getting the point.

"They was hit," Moran asserted vigorously. "Feller told me was with Ajax's outfit on the road, an' he wasn't an Ajax man. Said this bunch hopped on 'em at Elbow Creek, but they didn't like the guns o' the Ajax men. Hung around a while an' then beat it."

Green nodded. "That's right, Tom," he said.

"Figured I'd tell you," Moran mumbled. "News is goin' all over town now."

Kern said, "Glad you told us, Tom."

Moran went out, still a little puzzled, and Everett Green rubbed out his cigar in the ash tray. He stood up, hitching at his trousers, and he said quietly, "Didn't you see that coming, Kern?"

"Should have seen it," Kern said.

"Bovard's behind all of it," Green scowled. "He's running this trail-pirate bunch. He organized them, and he's hitting at every outfit on the road. He has to hit at his own wagons to throw suspicion off himself. Now that there's been an attack on an Ajax outfit, nobody can says he's in with them."

"That's logical," Kern agreed. "Now prove it."

"Can't prove a damned thing," Green muttered, and he walked over to the street window to look out. He stood there for some time, frowning, hands deep in his pockets. Then he said, "If it keeps up, Bovard's crews will be the only ones on the trail. They'll get all the orders because everybody else will be holed up in town here afraid to go out. The shippers will be afraid to trust the other outfits with cargos, but they'll have confidence in Ajax Overland because they're getting through."

"Even though they're hit, too," Kern murmured, "by fake raids."

"If Bovard can't buy or scare his competitors out of business," Green said bitterly, "or beat them senseless with his cut rates, he brings in his trail pirates to burn them up and slaughter their teamsters."

"He hasn't hurt us yet," Kern stated. "We have that Fort McLane contract assured if I can reach McLane in fifteen days with that big load. That contract alone can keep us in business."

"We don't have the McLane contract yet," Green reminded him. "The *Robert Grimes* is still far down the river. She's not due here till the middle of September or the end of the month."

"Plenty of time to get out to McLane before the bad weather sets in," Kern said confidently.

Everett Green didn't say anything for a few moments, and then he swung around from the window. He said quietly, "You know, don't you, that Rocky Mountain Freighting is holding up the other freight outfits in this town? They're still in the fight because another pretty big outfit is bucking Ajax Overland. When you go down they'll give up the ghost in twenty-four hours.

That means Ajax has a monopoly, and you know what that means."

"I know," Kern nodded. "We don't intend to go down."

"You're in a bigger fight than for just Rocky Mountain Freighting Company," Green told him slowly. "There's more at stake than dollars and cents and contracts and freight hauls. This is big, Kern."

Kern looked at him steadily. "I know how big it is," he said.

Green smiled a little. "I knew your Uncle Billy for a long time," he observed. "He was the best freighting man in this country. He made the trails and he organized the business. He could talk Indian tribes into letting him roll through their hunting grounds. Right now, though, I'm glad Billy McCloud isn't running this outfit. We need a different kind of man now, Kern. We need your kind of man."

Kern didn't say anything. He sat there, smoking the cigar, and then he heard Everett Green say from the window, "New girl in town, Kern. You seen her?"

"No," Kern said. He was thinking of Ajax Overland, of Bovard, of the big haul he had to make out to Fort McLane within a few weeks.

"Noticed her this morning," Green, who was not a lady's man, said casually. "Have a look, Kern."

Kern stepped to the window and looked out. She was coming down past the Rocky Mountain office. Her dress was of dull green silk, the bodice trimmed with black lace. She wore a small black bonnet with tiny roses. Her black hair was done in ringlets. She stepped along the rough boardwalk daintily, heading toward the shopping district, and as she went past Kern Harlan suddenly became conscious of the fact that there was something quite familiar about her. He felt that he should have known her; that he'd met her somewhere before.

Everett Green was saying dryly, "Quite a beautiful young lady, Kern. Wonder what she's doing in Nebraska City."

Kern shook his head. He was frowning, knitting his brow, as she went by. She was fully as beautiful as Daphne Paxton, but in a different kind of way. This girl was darker. Her skin was almost brown, tanned, but Kern realized that that was ridiculous. Girls of her type did not have tanned faces. They avoided the sun as if it were the plague.

"Looks kind of familiar," Green drawled. "Now, if I didn't know the Steele family pretty well, I'd say that Jennifer Steele had a sister."

Kern gulped. "Jennifer!" he blurted out, and then he bolted for the door and raced down the steps. He came up behind the girl in the green costume just as she was slowing down to look into the window of a dress shop. "Jennifer!" Kern gasped. "Jennifer Steele!"

She turned around slowly, smiling a little at him. She said quietly, "What's all the excitement, Kern?"

Kern stood there gaping, looking at her dress, her hat, the green gloves on her hands, the tiny silver slippers protruding from beneath the flowing silk skirt. He remembered that in all of his life he'd never seen Jennifer Steele in a dress, and especially not a dress like this. Her clothing was as rich, as stylish, as expensive as Daphne Paxton's.

"I—I don't understand," Kern mumbled. "You leaving Nebraska City?"

"No," Jennifer said. She stood there, a parasol dangling from her fingertips, looking at him calmly. She'd changed again. Her hazel eyes seemed darker, deeper, and looking into them Kern Harlan was reminded of a tigress.

"Hardly recognized you," Kern told her.

"Any objections to my wearing a dress?" Jennifer smiled. She smiled with her face only. There was no smile in her eyes, and Kern had the feeling that she never again would smile with her eyes, that she was dead inside.

"You've changed," Kern told her. "I didn't recognize you from the window."

"I'm wearing women's clothes," Jennifer said.

He wanted to ask her why, but he knew that he

had no reason to put questions to her. His was idle curiosity, and it was no concern of his how she dressed.

He noticed that men passing by on the walk turned to stare at her. There were other women in Nebraska City, plenty of women, but not her type, or Daphne Paxton's type.

"I just wanted to say," Kern murmured, "that you look very attractive in that outfit, and that you ought to dress up more often."

"Thank you," Jennifer said.

Kern stepped aside, realizing that he was making himself look quite ridiculous standing there. He said, "Glad you're staying in town, Jennifer."

"I have no intention of leaving Nebraska City," Jennifer told him, "just yet."

She passed on, the green silk dress swishing lightly as she walked. Kern went back to the office in a daze. Everett Green was smoking his cigar, still standing by the window, looking out.

Kern said to him, as if he still didn't quite believe it, "Everett, that was Jennifer Steele—Jack's sister."

"I know whose sister she is," Green said dryly.

Kern sat down limply behind his desk. He said, "What do you make of it, Everett? You've known Jennifer as long as I have."

The commissary shrugged. "Usually, when a woman dresses up she's after a man," he said.

Kern shook his head. "She's not," he said. "I know."

Green turned from the window and leaned against the wall, the cigar dangling a little. His eyes were narrowed, speculative. He said, "How do you know, Kern?"

Kern looked at him and shook his head again. "I know," he murmured.

Everett Green took the cigar from his mouth and tossed it into a spittoon near the wall. He said softly, "You and I are on two different streets, Kern. I still think she's after a man."

"She's not the kind who makes a play for a man," Kern said stubbornly. "I've known her since she was a child."

The commissary sauntered toward the door. He paused there just before going out, and he said gently, "I didn't say making a play for a man, Kern. I said that she was *after* a man."

He went out then, and Kern stared after him, a cold chill beginning to run through him as the significance of Everett Green's words sank into him. Jennifer was *after* a man. She was the tigress, stalking someone, stalking someone whom she hated, whom she wanted to kill, someone who had hurt her. Although no one could prove it, she knew, and Kern knew, that the man responsible for the death of her brother was Trace Bovard. The man she was stalking, then, was Trace Bovard.

Kern sat there glumly, knowing that there was nothing he could say or do in this matter. He knew Jennifer Steele. She had a mind of her own, and she would go through with this thing to the bitter end. She would even destroy herself in destroying Bovard.

Burton Reeves came in, a letter in his thin, ink-stained hand. He placed the letter on the desk in front of Kern and said, "Denver Mining Company wants to hold up that shipment of machinery that just came in on the *Lucy Belle*. They'll hold it in a local warehouse until the trail is safer."

Kern frowned. He looked at the letter and then tossed it aside. He said tersely, "We needed that haul, Reeves."

Reeves nodded. Looking up at him suddenly, Kern fancied that there was a gleam of triumph in the man's eyes. It disappeared quickly if it had been there.

Reeves said, "We need ready cash, Harlan. Buying out Steele put us in a hole."

"It was a good investment," Kern growled. "We needed that extra stock and equipment."

"We won't need anything," Reeves murmured, "if the trail is closed by trail bandits and every shipper is afraid to let a cargo leave Nebraska City."

"The trail won't be closed very long," Kern said tersely.

"I understand they hit at an Ajax outfit," Reeves murmured.

Kern nodded. "That's the rumor," he said. He pushed his chair back and stood up. He said, "What about that consignment for Burnett Brothers up on Winfield Creek?"

Burton Reeves looked at his hands. "John Burnett is in town," he said. "You can see him, but they're still a little afraid."

"Staple goods," Kern scowled. "You'd think they'd be anxious to get the stuff up there."

"Nonperishables," Reeves shrugged. "They'd rather get their cargo through late than not at all."

"It'll get through," Kern said grimly. "I'll take it myself."

He was fed up with this inactivity, this trying to wheedle shippers into rolling their cargos. He was sick of the office and of the town and he wanted to be out on the road again, pushing his bulls. He had intended to wait until the Fort McLane shipment came through, and then take out that big load himself, but the steamer bringing up the post's winter supplies had been delayed, and there was plenty of time to run up to Winfield Creek with the Burnett consignment and get back before the *Robert Grimes* docked.

"About forty ton on that consignment," Reeves murmured. "About eight wagons."

Kern put on his hat and went out into the yard.

He located Tom Moran and Bull Shannon in the blacksmith shop.

Moran said, "You see Jennifer Steele, Kern?"

"I saw her," Kern said briefly.

"Bird o' paradise," Moran grinned. "Never knew she was such a good-looker, did you, Kern?"

"No," Kern agreed. "We have eight or ten wagons ready to roll, Tom?"

"Plenty o' wagons," Moran nodded. "No damn shippers with guts." He grinned at Shannon, and the Bull nodded vigorously.

"I'm seeing John Burnett about his consignment up to Winfield Creek," Kern told him. "Have those wagons ready, Tom. If I can talk Burnett into it, we'll load up tonight and roll in the morning."

Moran said, "Shannon?"

Kern shook his head. "I'll take this myself," he said. "I want you and Shannon along, with about a dozen extra men as escort. We'll need that many to convince Burnett we can get through."

"We'll get through," Bull Shannon growled. "They ain't stoppin' Rocky Mountain wagons."

Moran said casually, "That office cagin' you in, Kern?"

"I'll feel better on the road," Kern admitted, smiling a little.

Shannon grunted and rubbed his nose vigorously. "Only place for a man," he agreed. "Open country, rollin' wagons."

Moran said, "We'll have the wagons an' men ready in the yard, Kern. Good luck."

Kern left the yard, walking downtown. It was about five o'clock in the afternoon now, and if he knew John Burnett of Burnett Brothers, the man would be in the Alhambra Saloon having a drink before supper. The Burnetts were old customers of Uncle Billy McCloud, and they'd been shipping through Rocky Mountain Freighting for more than a dozen years. The consignment of foodstuffs, cloth, and hardware was destined for Winfield Creek, a new settlement about eighty miles northwest of Nebraska City. It was a five-day trip with a good trail and no bad crossings to make.

Crossing the dusty road to the Alhambra, with the late September sun still hot, though low in the sky, Kern saw Jennifer Steele coming out of a hat shop. She had a hatbox dangling from her fingertips. She'd bought a new hat, another one to go with that fetching little bonnet with the tiny roses and the green ribbon. All of her life Jennifer had worn the flat-crowned sombreros worn by the men on the trail. She had never been too particular about her hair, either, yet she must have spent hours fixing up those little ringlets.

He watched as she passed on up the street, and he hoped fervently that Everett Green had been wrong, and that she had no deadly designs on Trace Bovard.

The heavy-set, red-faced John Burnett was at the bar inside the Alhambra when Kern came in. There were other men at the bar, also, about a half dozen of them scattered here and there. Trace Bovard stood with two men at the far end, and seeing him, Kern frowned a little.

Burnett waved a big hand when Kern came up. He said, "On me, Harlan." He poured the drink without even waiting for Kern's answer.

Kern said to him as he lifted the glass, "You're getting old, John. You spend too much time in your office now."

Burnett looked at him, uncertainty in his blue eyes. "How so, Kern?" he asked.

"You let trail pirates hold up your shipments." Kern smiled at him challengingly. "Ten years ago you wouldn't have done that, John."

John Burnett frowned. "Easy to talk," he scowled. "We have ten thousand dollars' worth of staples down on the wharf, Kern. Why should we risk it?"

"I'm willing to risk eight wagons and fifty-odd head of cattle," Kern told him, "and I'll bet you a hundred dollars I can afford it less than you."

Burnett looked at him, and then at the half-empty glass in his hand. He said stubbornly, "Whole town's holding up shipments, Kern, since this crew started its raids."

Kern put his glass back on the bar. "Been raids," he admitted. "You hear of any Rocky Mountain wagons being burned?"

"No," Burnett admitted.

"We're still rolling," Kern told him quietly, "if we can get anybody to put their cargos in our wagons. We'll guarantee delivery, too."

Burnett moistened his thick lips. He said slowly, "Damned stuff is needed up there at Winfield. Our warehouse is pretty near empty." He pushed his glass away from him and took out a cigar. Biting off the tip, he put the cigar in his mouth and lighted it. He said, "How can you guarantee delivery? Not a freight man in town will make that promise after all these raids."

"I'm taking this outfit up to Winfield myself," Kern told him. "It's going through."

John Burnett said touchily, "You didn't tell me that a few days ago. That's another story."

"We can load you tonight," Kern told him, "and move out at dawn. We'll have your stuff in Winfield in five days or I'll quit the freighting business, John."

John Burnett nodded. "You have a consignment, Harlan," he said evenly. "Load up." He had a heavy voice that carried, and as he said this Trace Bovard turned around at the other end of the bar to look down at them.

Kern stepped to the barroom door. O'Keefe, the teamster, was just moving past the front of the establishment, leading a yoke of oxen down to the Rocky Mountain yard. Kern called to him, "Tell Everett Green to load up that Burnett cargo. We're rolling in the morning."

O'Keefe nodded and grinned. He kept going, the dull-eyed oxen plodding after him.

Kern went back to the bar. He said to John Burnett, "Reckon this whole town's getting pretty tired of this outlaw bunch. If it keeps up we'll have to start a vigilante committee to work on them. I have a feeling that they make their headquarters right here in Nebraska City; that they get their orders from this point, too."

Bovard had turned around and was facing them directly now. Kern had intentionally raised his voice so that not only Bovard but the other men in the room heard his remarks.

Burnett was saying grimly, "If this bunch is operating from here, Harlan, we certainly need a vigilante committee."

Bovard came down along the bar, one hand resting on the wood as he walked, caressing it gently. He stopped on the other side of Burnett, and he said evenly, "How would you know, Mr. Harlan, that these trail pirates are operating from Nebraska City?"

"For one reason," Kern told him, "they seem to know which outfits to hit and which to let alone. They pick out the small outfits. How would they know that unless they had spies in Nebraska

City, checking up on every bull outfit leaving town?"

Trace Bovard nodded amiably. "Any other reasons?" he wanted to know.

"Some," Kern said coldly. "This town is full of strangers."

"Is that bad?" Bovard asked grimly. "I'm a stranger myself."

Kern shrugged. He smiled, but he said nothing, leaving the burden on Bovard. He saw the red come into the man's wide, fleshy face. Bovard's cool green eyes were smoldering as he stood at the bar, one powerful hand resting on the wood, solid legs spread slightly. He said slowly:

"Harlan, you've been asking for trouble for a long time in this town."

"I never ask for it," Kern observed, "nor do I run away from it, Bovard. Remember that."

He pushed away from the bar then, knowing that sooner or later he would have it out with the owner of Ajax Overland. Very possibly tonight was the night.

Out on the porch he stood there, lighting a cigar, giving Bovard plenty of time to think about it and to make up his mind. He leaned against one of the porch pillars, the cigar in his mouth, hands in his pockets, knowing that Bovard could see him over the tops of the batwing doors.

John Burnett came out first. He paused beside Kern and said, "Reckon you got yourself a fight tonight, Kern, if that's what you were looking for."

Kern shrugged and smiled. "Never liked that man," he murmured.

"Hate to tackle him, myself," Burnett stated. "He looks like he could be rough."

"I'm rough, too," Kern said.

Burnett smiled a little. "Sure," he said. Then he moved away to the other porch pillar, saying softly, "Here it comes."

Kern heard the batwing doors squeak slightly as Trace Bovard came out. He saw the man's bulky shadow on the walk below him, the breadth of his shoulders, and then he turned his head.

Bovard said, "You make a remark, Harlan, and then you run outside."

"Cleaner air out here," Kern stated.

Across the road two men who had been talking turned around to stare at them. The other drinkers inside the Alhambra were coming out, pushing through the doors, moving along the porch, their boots making the boards squeak.

The late-afternoon sun shining in under the west end of the porch threw Bovard's shadow on the walk directly below Kern, and Kern watched that shadow and not the man. He smoked his cigar, leaning carelessly against the post. It was hot at this hour, although an hour from now, when the sun was gone, it would be quite cool.

A buckboard rolled past the saloon, the driver

almost dozing on the seat. Then he glanced toward the porch, and seeing Kern and Bovard standing a few feet apart, he suddenly sat upright, turned his buckboard in toward the nearest tie rack, and leaped to the ground.

Trace Bovard said softly, "I'm not Bull Shannon, Harlan. I'm not a stupid ox driver."

Kern turned his head slightly to look at him. He smiled again, that cool, calculating smile that seemed to upset Bovard so much. He didn't say anything, but it was worse than any insult he could have directed at Bovard. That smile was the match that ignited the powder.

Bovard stepped up closer and shoved out his right arm violently, hitting Kern behind the left shoulder with the open palm of his hand, propelling him off the porch.

It was two steps to the rough boardwalk below. Kern landed lightly on both feet, and even as he landed he was calmly stripping off his coat. Bovard came off the porch in a flying leap, much faster than Kern had expected him, and Kern had to step nimbly to avoid him and get his arms clear of the coat.

He backed into the dusty road, tossing the coat across the tie rack as he did so.

A man on the walk was yelling excitedly, "Ajax! Ajax!"

It was the rallying call for all Ajax Overland men in the vicinity. Trace Bovard, about to plunge in with both fists, stopped suddenly. He pointed a thick finger at the Ajax man and he said tersely, "Stay out of this. Every one of you. He's mine."

Kern waited for him, and he rubbed his hands easily on the sides of his pants. Trace Bovard had been right when he said that he was not Bull Shannon. The Bull was awesomely strong, a bigger, heavier man than Bovard, but he did not have Bovard's brain or his indomitable will. Watching him move in, Kern had the queer feeling that Trace Bovard would not cease fighting until he was dead. He would take punishment far beyond anything Shannon had taken, and still move forward.

The Ajax head lunged in, arms swinging, big shoulders hunched, his wide face set tight, cold green eyes deep in his head. Kern moved away from him, watching carefully. He was somewhat taller than Bovard, but he didn't have Bovard's bulk or physical strength. His fight this afternoon was to hit and retreat until Bovard could no longer carry the fight, and then to go on the offensive.

He hit Bovard full in the mouth with a swinging fist, splitting the man's lips, sending the blood gushing down his shirt front. Bovard came on as if he'd been brushed across the mouth with a feather duster.

A hard blow caught Kern high on the side of

the face and he staggered. He saw the triumph well up in Bovard's green eyes as the big man rushed in to grapple with him, and he knew then what kind of fight this would be. Bull Shannon had wanted a straight, stand-up fight, a clean fight. Bovard wanted to win, to destroy, to kill. He did not care how he did it. Once he got his man down on the ground he would never let him up again.

Kern righted himself, stepped away from Bovard's rush, and then swung his left fist hard into the man's stomach. There was a dull thump, but no appreciable slackening of Bovard's drive. He was hard down there, too, like a bass drum.

They fought more slowly now, eying each other carefully as the crowd gathered. It was not a noisy crowd, either, as there had been at the Shannon fight. They watched silently as the two fighters circled each other.

Bovard suddenly tore in again, and Kern, instead of backing away and snapping a fist into Bovard's face as he had been doing, stepped in and hit the Ajax man squarely on the jaw with his right fist.

Trace Bovard's head went up. He stiffened, arms at his sides, and for one moment Kern thought he was going down. Stepping in, he hit Bovard twice more, hard, slashing blows to the face, tearing the flesh, but these blows seemed to revive Bovard rather than rendering him unconscious. He steadied himself and started to walk in slowly.

Kern heard a sigh go up from the big circle of watching men. Blood streamed down Bovard's face from a half-dozen cuts. His mouth was pulverized. The flesh over his left eye was loose, hanging. His shirt front was red with blood, but he walked in.

Thinking of Jack Steele, Kern felt no pity for the man. He continued to hit out hard, savagely, as he retreated from Bovard's rushes, and then occasionally he would stop and swing, both men standing there, arms pumping.

He'd been hit hard a number of times himself. Blood dripped down from the right side of his face where Bovard's fist had raked the flesh. His ribs hurt from the slashing Bovard had given him, and he hoped that none of them had been broken.

The long shadows fell across the street, across the two fighters in the circle of watching men. The late sun gleamed red on the windows facing west, and then a cooling breeze sprang up.

They fought silently, intently, Bovard never ceasing to lunge in, Kern avoiding his rushes. Once Kern slipped as he backed away, and as he fell, Bovard, eyes flaming through the mass of bruised and bleeding flesh, dove at him.

Rolling, Kern kicked savagely, rolled again, and came up on his knees. Bovard scrambled to his feet, too, like a big cat, and then kicked at

Kern's face with his right foot. There was enough power in that kick to fracture Kern's skull had it landed.

Turning his head slightly, Kern shot out his right hand. He grasped Bovard's ankle, jerked hard, and dropped the man in the dust beside him. He got up then, dusting himself, noticing for the first time how far the sun had fallen in the sky. They were in complete shadow now, and he realized that they had been fighting for nearly an hour. It was time to think about ending it. It was inconceivable that Bovard could have much strength left in his massive frame after the beating he had been taking.

He was still coming in. He lunged, and Kern hit him in the mouth again, and then he hit again, and again. For the first time Bovard took a backward step. He did not take it voluntarily. The force of Kern's blows drove him back toward the tie rack, and the crowd began to hum excitedly.

Kern moved in now, hitting with both fists, hard, heavy, slogging blows to the face and to the body, driving Bovard before him, and then Bovard stopped. His right eye was completely closed, and had been closing for some time. His left was puffed, and very shortly that would be closed, too, so that he would be completely blinded.

He stood there, dumbly, and then he reached out for the tie rack and held it with his left hand, steadying himself, feeling for Kern with the right.

Sickened at the sight, Kern held up. Bovard would not go down. He stood there, holding himself up with his hand on the rail. Kern hit him again, and he reached with his other hand and gripped the rail with both hands, his face still lifted for the punishment.

Kern looked at him, and then turned and pushed through the crowd and up the steps into the saloon. Trace Bovard would stand there all night. He knew that; he would never go down to the ground. He would die that way, on his feet.

The bartender of the Alhambra was standing to one side of the doors as Kern went past him, and Kern mumbled, "Harry, I need a drink."

"Reckon we all do, Kern," the bartender murmured. "He's a tough one."

John Burnett came in and stood beside Kern as he had his drink at the bar. He said quietly, "Still feel like rolling freight, Kern?"

Kern nodded. He looked at his hands. They were swollen, puffed, bruised. His face was not much better, and his ribs felt as if he'd been kicked by a horse.

Burnett said thoughtfully, "You let that man alone, Kern, and he'll run the freighting industry in this country. He's like that."

"I know it," Kern agreed, and then he added, "We're not letting him alone, John. You can bet on that."

Chapter Nine

The Rocky Mountain wagons were rolling at dawn, nine wagons moving through the dim, murky light, sleepy-eyed bullwhackers striding beside the wagons, the teams of oxen surging into the harness, an occasional bull whip cracking, and then mumbled curses.

The big wagons rumbled heavily, wheels sinking deep into the dust of the road. Drunks reeling out of the now dimly lighted saloons stared at the wagons stupidly as they went by.

Kern rode at the head of the column, his face and hands still sore from the fight. He wondered how Bovard felt this morning. He'd seen the Ajax owner being led away by two employees, led like a blind man, walking stolidly, his legs still strong beneath him.

Tom Moran and a dozen Rocky Mountain men rode with Kern, forming the escort for this bull outfit. With the cook and the three night herders, there were twenty-seven armed men in the party, a fairly formidable force.

It was still dark when they rolled into the ox trail, but the stars were thinning and losing their brilliance. There was light in the eastern sky, and it was quite cold. Already Kern Harlan could sense the quick approach of winter—the dreaded

Midwestern winter with the blankets of snow and the freezing, bitter cold. He could smell it in the air, even though by high noon this day would be hot.

Moran rode up to his side and said laconically, "How do you feel this mornin', Kern?"

"Like I'd been put through a wringer," Kern smiled wryly.

Moran nodded. "Lot more fun fightin' Shannon, I'd imagine."

"It was," Kern agreed. "There's no humor in Trace Bovard."

"Didn't figure there was," Tom Moran grinned. "He'll try to break you now, Kern, if he has to wreck his own line to do it. You watch him."

"I'll watch him," Kern nodded, and he realized that Moran was speaking the truth. Bovard was a man with pride, and that pride had been humbled; not beaten into the dust, but he'd been humbled and he knew it. He'd never rest in this world until he'd evened up the score.

Moran fell back again with the escort, and Kern rode on silently, listening to the familiar sounds behind him, the clank of ox chains and the loose rattle of brake blocks, the occasional snort of a horse, and then the rumble of the big, heavily loaded wagons.

He thought then of Jennifer Steele, wondering what she would do, how far she would go in her plans. He wondered if it were possible that they'd been mistaken about Jennifer, and that she really had no deadly designs on Bovard because of the death of her brother. Remembering that look in her eyes, though, he knew that they had not been mistaken.

It was cool and brisk when the sun came up, and the clear plains air put the men in good spirits. They broke out into song as they came down a grade, and Kern Harlan listened, a slight smile on his face, remembering that song, thinking of the first time he'd heard it, riding proudly beside Uncle Billy McCloud, a small boy of eight.

> "I'll tell you how it is when
> You first get on the road.
> You have an awkward team and
> A very heavy load.
>
> "You have to whip and holler, but
> Swear upon the sly.
> You're in for it then, boys,
> Root hog or die!"

He had to root now or he would surely die. His back was up against the wall, financially, and he had to fight his way out of it. He had to get this load through to prove that Rocky Mountain wagons could defy the trail pirates, and he had to get that Fort McLane cargo through in the allotted time.

After the noonday rest, he sent Moran and Shannon up ahead as point riders, and he called off a rear-guard detail of five men. Other riders were out on the wings, and they rolled along like an army detachment.

At night a heavy guard was set out and the stock permitted to graze and then driven inside the enclosure. Heavy logging chains were drawn across the opening and temporary barricades set up.

Tom Moran said with a satisfied air, "Reckon they won't be botherin' us much, Kern. This is a regular hornet's nest."

"We'll sting them if they come," Kern said.

In the morning the clear weather turned bad. Rain came up out of the east, a chill, drizzling rain. Kern tied a poncho around his shoulders, but most of the bullwhackers just strode along beside their wagons, sloshing through the mud that quickly formed in the trail, oblivious of the weather.

Crossing Squaw Creek they had to double team because the mud was thick on both sides of the creek. One wagon was nearly upset as it rolled out of the swollen creek. Kern held his breath as the heavy wagon righted itself and came onto more solid ground.

He called an early halt that afternoon because the oxen had had a hard day of it and needed the extra rest. It had been an uneventful day. As yet they'd seen no signs of the trail pirates, and Kern was inclined to agree with Tom Moran that they wouldn't bother this strongly armed outfit.

In the morning there was a frost, the first real hint of the coming winter. The sun quickly dispelled the frost, drying up the trail again, and they made good time this third day, camping at Pillow Rock.

Kern rode on ahead that afternoon to shoot two buffalo cows, providing fresh meat for the men at the evening meal. Again the same precautions were taken, the stock driven inside the wagon corral at dusk and the heavy guard set out.

The fourth day they spotted a band of Sioux crossing their trail about noon. There were women and children with this band, and Kern slowed down his wagons until they were out of sight behind the ridges.

The afternoon of the fifth day they rolled into the tiny hamlet of Winfield Creek, a straggling string of houses, a few saloons, log huts, and a warehouse along the creek. Winfield was the supply center for the ranchers and nesters who were beginning to open up this section of the country.

Men came out of the houses and saloons to cheer as the ten big wagons rolled down to the Burnett Brothers warehouse to unload. Jacob Burnett, the other brother of the company, rubbed his chin thoughtfully as he came out of his office adjoining the warehouse. Unlike his brother, Jacob Burnett was short and fat with a wide, fleshy face.

He said to Kern, "John told me he was going to hold up this shipment, Harlan."

"Changed his mind," Kern said briefly. "We're here."

"I'm glad to see you," the brother said. "We're looking for a tough winter out here, and I'd rather see this stuff in my warehouse than lying on the wharf in Nebraska City. Have any trouble?"

"No trouble," Kern told him. "We came right through."

Jacob Burnett looked at the wagons and at the crew. He said, "Pretty big crew for ten wagons, Kern. Reckon that's why they didn't bother you."

"I told John we'd get these wagons through," Kern stated.

"You're lucky," Jacob Burnett smiled. "Every freight outfit can't afford to double its crew on every haul and make a profit."

"We can't either, indefinitely," Kern said dryly. "That pirate crew will have to be stopped."

"How?" Burnett asked. "There's no real law and order in this country yet. We could appeal to the military, but they have their hands full, I believe, keeping the Indians in line. Besides, this isn't an ordinary band of cutthroats. I wouldn't be surprised if they broke up after each raid and came back into the settlements. The

Army would be chasing so much quicksilver."

"We'll have to do it ourselves," Kern told him, "or the day of free freighting is over."

He ate with Jacob Burnett that night in the only eating place in town, a small lunchroom off the bar of the Arrowhead Saloon. From the table where they sat smoking cigars after the meal he could look into the barroom. Moran, Shannon, and a few other Rocky Mountain teamsters were at the bar, with Moran keeping an eye on the men to see that they did not consume too much liquor.

With the wagons unloaded, Kern had given them orders to be ready to pull out in the morning for the return trip. Shannon was engaged in a friendly argument with one of the Rocky Mountain men, and then the two of them stood up to the bar and placed elbows on the wood, Shannon's left and the other teamster's right. They engaged in a friendly little contest, each man trying to throw the other with the pressure of the arm.

Hands clasped, they braced themselves and strained. The face of the teamster engaging Bull Shannon became red with the effort, but Shannon grinned easily as he bent his man farther and farther backward.

A small crowd had gathered to watch the contest, and they formed a ring around the two men. Kern watched the feat of strength as he puffed on his cigar. His eyes moved across the faces of the spectators, coming to rest on a broad face with a flattened nose and high Indian cheekbones. The man's hair was brown and long. He had weasel's eyes, small, reddish, close-set.

For one moment Kern looked away from this man, and then his eyes moved back again to that wide, flat-nosed face. He had the feeling that he should have known this man, that he'd run across him only a short time before. He sat there, a small frown on his face, wondering why he could not connect the man with the incident, and then suddenly he knew. The last time he'd seen this man he'd had stripes painted across his face. He'd been riding away from the raid on Bull Shannon's wagons, and he'd pointed a pistol in Kern's face, pulling the trigger on an empty chamber. The man was one of the trail crew preying upon the bull outfits.

Kern took the cigar from his mouth, rubbed it out in the plate in front of him, and stood up. He said to Jacob Burnett, "I'll have a drink with the boys. Mind if I bunk in the warehouse tonight?"

"Not at all," Burnett said. "No hotels in this town."

They shook hands, Burnett going back to his office, Kern moving through the open doorway into the barroom. Bull Shannon had the Rocky Mountain teamster bent back so far now that he could no longer maintain his balance. With a gasp he staggered away from the bar, Shannon releasing his grip on the man's hand.

Kern caught him as he lurched his way, righting him again. He said to Shannon, smilingly, "I'm next, Bull."

"Come to it," Shannon invited.

Kern placed his right elbow on the bar, his hand upraised. Shannon grasped the hand, braced himself on the bar floor, and grinned at Kern. He said, "Ready?"

Kern nodded. He didn't expect to beat the big bullwhacker in this contest. Shannon was known as the strongest man on the trail, and he'd never been bested in a contest of strength like this one.

They put the pressure on, Shannon using his left arm, the weaker arm, and giving Kern the advantage. For one moment Kern started to bend the big man's arm backward across the top of the bar. He put everything he had into the pressure, moving Shannon's wrist back about two inches, and then the giant held.

Shannon was still grinning as he started to bring his hand upright again, very slowly, until both locked hands were in a perpendicular position. Then Shannon's arm started to move the other way, bending Kern's arm backward.

For fully five minutes Kern resisted the pressure, the sweat breaking out on his face. A bigger crowd had gathered around them to watch, and a few bets were made.

Tom Moran said, "No use, Kern. He's got iron in his arm. He nearly killed me last week."

Kern held it as long as he could, and then he gave way, staggering away from the bar when Shannon released him. He came back to the bar, rubbing his arm, and then he slapped Shannon's back. He said, "I owe you a drink, Shannon."

"Sure," the Bull grinned. Looking around the room, he boomed, "Who's next?"

There were no takers. The bartender took a bottle from the shelf and set it down in front of Kern, along with two glasses. Kern looked at the bottle and then turned around. The man with the flattened nose was just turning away and the group beginning to disperse.

Kern said to the flat-nosed man, "Why don't you try him, friend?"

The man shook his head and grinned, revealing yellowed teeth. He said, "Not me, Jack."

"Why not?" Kern asked him.

The flat-nosed man frowned. He said tersely, "Your business, mister?"

Tom Moran was looking at Kern curiously, wondering why he was deliberately fostering an argument on this man.

Kern said casually, "Maybe I'm just curious. What's your name?"

The man moistened his lips as if deliberating whether he should answer the question. He said coolly, "Brown."

Kern turned to face him. He said gently, "Why don't you want to try this, Brown?"

Brown looked at him, his weasel eyes narrowed. He said, "Hell with you, mister."

Kern put his hands in his vest pockets and leaned back against the bar, smiling coldly now. He said, "Maybe it's because you're tired, Brown. Maybe you were out with your crew last night—raiding bull outfits."

The man's face took on a mottled hue. He licked his lips, and his eyes started to rove around the room. Bull Shannon had stiffened at Kern's elbow. Tom Moran came away from the bar suddenly to have another look at the man.

Brown said thickly, "You're crazy, mister. I just come in from Denver. Been doin' some minin'. I kin prove it."

"Denver's a long way off," Kern murmured. "Who sent you out on those raids?"

Brown's face was a sickly color, and the fear was in his eyes, deep down, the fear of a coyote caught in a trap. He said, "Ain't been on no raids, mister. You got the wrong man."

He turned away and started to walk toward the door. Tom Moran caught up with him in two long strides, grasped him by the left shoulder, spun him around, and sent him whirling back up against the bar. He hit the wood with a resounding thud.

Moran said tersely, "Walk the other way, mister."

He stood against the bar, gripping it with his hands. Moran was standing in front of him, Kern to his right, and then Bull Shannon came away from the bar and moved up to stand with Moran. Brown had a gun on his hip, but he wasn't going to use it with three men in front of him.

Kern said softly, "I asked you a question, Brown. Who sent you on those raids?"

The crowd had gathered around again and was watching silently. Kern could hear the heavy breathing in the room. Brown didn't answer. He stood there, licking his lips, looking at Moran and Shannon in front of him.

Pouring a drink, Kern handed it to him. He said, "This might help you to remember, Brown. Drink it down."

The flat-nosed man looked at the glass. He made no attempt to take it from Kern's hand. Brushing the glass aside so that the liquor spilled to the floor, he made a ratlike leap forward, trying to dive between Moran and Shannon and scuttle for the door.

Shannon's big knee shot out, catching him on the side of the head, knocking him over in Moran's direction. Moran grasped him by the shoulders and whirled him back up against the bar again. The bar shook this time as he hit it. He stood there, dazed, slavering a little at the mouth.

Kern came around in front of him and grasped

his left arm by the elbow with both hands. He braced himself and called to Shannon behind him, "Take his right arm, Bull. We'll see if he can throw you."

Shannon came up, grinning, put his elbow on the wood, and grasped Brown's right hand as he had been doing in the other contests. Kern remained where he was, gripping the man's left arm so that he was backed up against the bar in an awkward position, his right elbow on the top of the bar, Shannon grasping his right hand in his own left.

Shannon said tersely, "Let him go, Kern. I'll make him wriggle."

Kern shook his head. "It'll break easier this way, Bull," he said. "Go ahead."

Shannon looked past Brown's ashen face at Kern. He said doubtfully, "Yeah?"

"Break it off," Kern told him calmly.

Brown gasped as Shannon started to apply the pressure. His right arm went back farther and farther, and the sweat broke out on his face. He struggled desperately to break loose, but Kern held him back against the bar so that he could not move while Shannon bent the arm.

A short scream broke from his lips, and Kern signaled for Shannon to let up a little. He said quietly, "Think you can remember now? Who sent you on those raids?"

The flat-nosed man was gasping, tears of pain

in his eyes. They still had him pinned against the bar, one man on either side. He opened his mouth, closed it, and then opened it again, knowing that it was useless trying to stall.

It was then that the shot came from the door. Very distinctly Kern Harlan heard the sickening whack of the bullet as it struck Brown's body. He felt the quick convulsion as Brown surged forward, and he knew that the bullet had been fatal.

Letting him fall, he whirled toward the door, sliding his gun from the holster. The bullet had passed between two spectators, probably grazing one of them, because he was holding his right arm near the elbow, a stunned expression on his face.

Kern dived through them, Shannon and Moran at his heels. He went through the batwing doors and out onto the rickety boardwalk in front of the saloon. Only a few seconds had elapsed from the time the shot had been fired until Kern was out on the walk, but in those seconds the murderer had disappeared.

Standing there, his gun tight in his fist, Kern listened. There were no sounds. He raced to the far end of the building and looked up the dark alley there. Moran and Shannon headed the other way, pausing at the mouth of the alley at that end. They came back, shaking their heads.

Kern said grimly, "He's gone. Could have run

across the road and into one of the houses over there."

"Didn't waste much time," Moran growled.

They went back into the saloon and over to the group around the man on the floor. Kern took one look at him and turned away. He frowned at Bull Shannon, and the Bull said:

"Reckon this one's no good either, Kern."

Chapter Ten

Back in Nebraska City after an uneventful trip, Kern had a haircut and a shave in the barbershop across from the Sherman Hotel. Everett Green came in as the barber was finishing up. He sat down in the empty chair next to Kern and he said:

"Any trouble?"

"We made it," Kern said succinctly. "Didn't figure they'd raid us, anyway." He looked at Green in the mirror on the wall and said, "What's new in Nebraska City?"

The commissary wrinkled his nose a little. "For one thing," he murmured, "I'd say Jennifer Steele has found herself a gentleman friend."

Kern looked at him, his lips tightening. He didn't say anything until they were outside, striding along the boardwalk toward the Rocky Mountain yard. Then he said shortly, "She's crazy."

Green nodded. He walked along, whistling softly.

Kern said to him, "I'll talk to her. It's Bovard, isn't it?"

"Been riding around in Bovard's carriage," Green told him. "Having occasional suppers with Bovard in the Sherman Hotel dining room. I'd say they were quite friendly."

"What can she expect to learn from Bovard?"

Kern snapped. "Does she think he'll tell her that he had her brother shot down?"

Everett Green shrugged. "Reckon she figures if she's in with his crowd she'll learn something sooner or later. If not from Bovard, from one of Bovard's friends. A woman has a way of finding out things, Kern."

"She's out of her mind," Kern growled. "She has some money now. She ought to marry and settle down. She has to forget about this business. I'm taking care of it."

Green smiled a little. "Not too many eligible men around this town for a girl like Jennifer," he observed. "Seems like you're kind of tied up, yourself."

Kern glanced at him. "Never mind me," he muttered.

"Sure," Green said. "Now, what happened up at Winfield Creek? Moran told me a little of it."

Kern explained briefly. He discovered that he wasn't so much concerned now about freighting and trail pirates. He was worried about Jennifer. She was going around with Bovard, riding in his carriage, having meals with him, probably going to the occasional dances held in town. He didn't like that.

As they were walking across the Rocky Mountain yard, Green said to him, "Wouldn't advise your trying to talk to Jennifer, Kern."

"Why not?" Kern demanded.

"She never listened to you before," Everett Green stated. "Why should she now?"

Kern didn't say anything to that. He strode in through the side door to the office, and as he went past Burton Reeves he said, "Any news yet on that McLane shipment?"

The office manager nodded. "Captain O'Hare of the *John Adams* told me this morning that the *Robert Grimes* is held up below St. Louis with a broken piston or something."

Kern scowled and shook his head.

Green said with attempted jocularity, "It looks like we'll have to roll that freight through the snow, Kern."

In the office Kern lighted a cigar and stood by the window, staring out, trouble in his eyes. This added delay on the big McLane shipment meant that he would have to wait that much longer for his pay for the haul, and he needed cash quickly. He wondered now if he'd made a mistake buying out the Steele line so quickly, and using up most of his available cash.

Green said, as if reading his thoughts, "Reckon you'll have to get a loan somewhere, Kern."

"Hate to borrow money," Kern scowled.

"Have anybody in mind you want to borrow it from?" Green asked him. "Or are you going to the bank?"

It was then that Kern thought of Tobias Paxton. Daphne's uncle evidently had money and he was looking for something in which to invest it. There was a possibility that Tobias might consider Rocky Mountain Freighting a good, sound investment.

"I'll have to look around," Kern said thoughtfully. "I'm not sure yet."

He asked Daphne Paxton to have dinner with him that evening, and when he saw Uncle Tobias coming across the hotel lobby he invited him to join them.

The portly, round-faced man was immaculately dressed, as usual, his short gray beard trimmed. Shaking hands warmly with Kern, he sat down at the table beside them.

"Saw your wagons rolling in, Mr. Harlan," Tobias Paxton smiled. "It appears that Rocky Mountain is the only freight outfit not afraid to put its wagons on the trail."

"We aim to keep the freight moving right up until the first heavy snow," Kern told him. "Rocky Mountain has always maintained that kind of service."

Uncle Tobias nodded. "An excellent policy, sir," he agreed. He started to order his meal, Kern watching him.

Daphne said suddenly, "Uncle, you should be engaged in some business in this town. There seems to be so much to do, and you have always had interests in other towns."

"Very true, my dear," Uncle Tobias smiled. "It will take time, of course, to make the proper connections. I have money to invest, but I haven't yet found the field for my few talents."

Kern said, "Have you ever considered the freighting business, Mr. Paxton?"

"Freight!" Tobias Paxton stared at him. "I know nothing of bulls and wagons and bullwhackers," he laughed.

Kern shrugged. "An investor needs only to know that a business is sound," he pointed out.

Daphne said, "Would you consider your own company a sound investment, Kern?"

Kern nodded. "We're the oldest freighting establishment in Nebraska City," he said. "I believe Rocky Mountain is considered one of the soundest companies in the West."

Tobias Paxton nodded. "Why are you telling me this?" he asked curiously.

Kern hesitated, and then wondered why he hesitated. Paxton was definitely interested. He had the money to invest, and money was what he, Kern Harlan, needed very badly in order to pay his help, to buy grain for his stock, to keep his wagons in condition. He said finally, "I am offering you an interest in Rocky Mountain Freight, Mr. Paxton. I feel that our company is a good investment."

Tobias Paxton looked at him thoughtfully, and then looked at his niece. Daphne was beaming.

She leaned forward across the table, her blue eyes sparkling.

"It would be wonderful, Uncle," she said. "Please do it."

Tobias Paxton smiled and rubbed his beard. He drummed with his fingers on the table for a moment, and then he said, "I would consider a partnership in Rocky Mountain Freighting, Mr. Harlan."

Kern stared at him, taken aback for the moment. He had not considered anything more than an investment in the company. A full partnership was something different.

Paxton laughed. He said, "Of course, this will be a silent partnership, Mr. Harlan. I know nothing of the freighting industry, and I will leave the complete management of the company to you. However, when I am prepared to invest as much as twenty or twenty-five thousand dollars, I feel that I should have a substantial interest in the company."

This too took Kern by surprise. The figure was about five times the amount of money he'd anticipated that Tobias Paxton would invest in Rocky Mountain Freighting. With twenty-five thousand dollars in cash he could expand and really compete with Ajax Overland. He could purchase some new wagons; he could expand his yard. In this present predicament he could furnish armed escorts with all his outfits, and keep his wagons rolling in spite of trail pirates or Indian troubles.

Daphne Paxton said pleadingly, "Please take us in, Kern."

Kern nodded. "I think it can be arranged," he said. "If you'll come over to my office in the morning, Mr. Paxton, we'll draw up a contract."

Tobias Paxton reached across the table and shook hands with him. He said, "It'll be a pleasure working with you, Mr. Harlan. You have an enviable reputation in this town. And now, if you'll excuse me, I'll leave you two young people to yourselves."

He pushed back his chair, and as Kern rose he saw Trace Bovard coming in with Jennifer Steele. They were both laughing, and Jennifer was holding Bovard's arm.

Daphne Paxton saw them, too, and she said curiously, "Your Miss Steele seems to have changed, Kern."

"She's changed," Kern scowled. He watched the two move across the dining room toward a corner table. Bovard held her chair as she sat down, and then he leaned over to take her wrap.

"You would think," Daphne said a little spitefully, "that after the death of her brother she would lead a more sensible life. She's making a hussy of herself."

Kern was on the point of defending Jennifer Steele. He opened his mouth to say something, and then closed it again. He was uncomfortable all the time that he was in the room with Bovard and Jennifer, and he was glad when he was able to say good night to Daphne in the lobby and step into the bar for a drink.

Standing at the bar, alone, face grim, he resolved that he would have his talk with Jennifer tonight. He owed that much to Jack Steele, who had been his friend.

As he was standing at the bar Everett Green came in and made his way directly toward him. Kern pushed the bottle toward him, but Green only shook his head.

The commissary said quietly, "Paxton is talking that he's going into partnership with you, Kern. Is that true?"

Kern looked at him, and then nodded. "Mr. Paxton wants to invest money," he stated. "I need the money. He's coming in as a silent partner. We're going to work out the details tomorrow."

Green took a deep breath. He said flatly, "I don't like it, Kern."

Kern looked at him steadily. He said softly, "Well."

Everett Green flushed a little, realizing that perhaps he'd gone too far. He said, "I'm not speaking as your commissary, Kern. I've been with Rocky Mountain for nineteen years now. I'm your friend, and I just don't like this."

"Why?" Kern asked bluntly.

Green shook his head. "I'm not sure why," he said. "I don't think it's a good policy to bring an outsider into the company. Uncle Billy built it up for you, Kern, not for some Easterner with a lot of money to invest."

"I need that money," Kern told him. "I'm hard up."

"You could have made a loan," Green stated. "There's a bank in this town would have loaned you money."

"Not that kind of money," Kern said. "I can make Rocky Mountain the biggest freighting outfit in the West."

Green looked at him steadily. He said, "That was not Uncle Billy's ideal, Kern."

"No?" Kern murmured.

"Billy McCloud thought only of service to the territory," Green said quietly. "He wasn't interested in size or in becoming the top man in the freighting industry."

Kern toyed with the glass on the bar in front of him. He said, "There's no service to the territory now with the trail practically closed by trail pirates. With money I can expand; I can furnish armed escorts when we need them, and I can keep the freight rolling no matter what happens. Wouldn't you call that service to the territory?"

Everett Green said stubbornly, "I just wish it could have been done some other way."

"You have any objections to Tobias Paxton, personally?" Kern asked him.

"Who knows Tobias Paxton?" Green countered. "He's a new face in Nebraska City. I'd go slow with strangers, Kern."

Kern laughed. "You worry too much, Everett," he said. "This is going to work out."

"I hope so," Green said moodily. "It's just that I wouldn't want an Easterner to come into the yard and give me orders."

"You'll take your orders from me," Kern assured him, "the same as usual."

Green went away after a while, and Kern stepped out on the street. It was past ten o'clock in the evening now, getting rather cold. He noticed that Bovard and Jennifer were still in the dining room even though the room was practically deserted at this late hour.

Out on the street he walked down toward the river. There were just a few boats tied up, looming white and ghostly out of the gloom. Huge piles of goods lay under tarpaulins, their owners afraid to ship because of the trail pirates. Occasional watchmen roamed along the wharf, rifles in their hands. They looked at Kern suspiciously. One man recognized him and said gruffly, "Gettin' cold, Mr. Harlan."

"That's right," Kern answered.

"They'd better be gettin' this stuff out o' here," the watchman growled, "afore the snow comes.

We had a big fall first part o' November last year. Remember?"

"I remember," Kern said. He knew, too, that sometimes the snow came even earlier than that, closing up the trails. Far away at Fort McLane hundreds of United States Army cavalrymen were waiting for the supplies now held up on the ill-fated *Robert Grimes* downriver. They needed this big cargo, and they were depending upon him to bring it through. He'd given the commanding officer his promise that he would deliver.

Standing there on the wharf, with the chill breeze coming off the dark river, he listened to the lapping of the water against the heavy timbers. He thought of Jennifer Steele back there, chatting gaily with Trace Bovard, and then of the evil in her heart.

He smoked a cigar halfway through, tossed it into the river, watched it sizzle out, and then turned back toward the town. Jennifer Steele lived in her brother's house on a quiet street not too far from Billy McCloud's big house. Kern knew the house well.

Walking up the street, past rows of wooden houses, the lights out in most of them now, he saw a carriage parked in front of the Steele house. Slowing down, he was about to turn back, knowing that the carriage was Trace Bovard's, and then he heard Bovard's gruff "Good night."

The carriage rolled off and Jennifer started up

the steps of the house. Increasing his pace again, Kern called quietly, "Jennifer."

Bovard's carriage turned at the corner and disappeared as Kern walked up to the house. Jennifer waited for him. She was wearing a dark blue evening cape, trimmed with fur, tied up tightly at the throat. Her hat was of dark blue material, too, very tiny, perched on the side of her head, a hat Jennifer Steele would have considered ridiculous a short time before.

"That you, Kern?" she asked.

There was a white picket fence in front of the house, and Kern opened the gate to step inside. She waited for him on the bottom step of the porch, and she said, "I see your wagons got through to Winfield. Congratulations."

Kern nodded. "Had no trouble," he said briefly. There was a slim sliver of moon tonight just swinging up over the tops of the houses across the road. The moonlight fell across her face as she stood on the step. It seemed to him that her face was pale, cold. He said, "I've been told you have a gentleman friend in Nebraska City, Jennifer."

Jennifer looked at him. "You're doing pretty well yourself, Kern," she told him.

Kern shook his head. "You're making a fool of yourself," he said gruffly. "What do you expect to gain from this, Jennifer?"

"From what?" Jennifer countered coolly.

Kern stared at her, for the first time in his life aware of the fact that Jennifer Steele was lovely. He said bluntly, "From this association with Trace Bovard—the man you think is responsible for the death of your brother."

Jennifer didn't say anything for a moment, and then she said stiffly, "Mr. Bovard is a friend of mine, Kern."

"You're a damned fool," Kern snapped. "He's a killer and you know it. He sent out that trail crew that wrecked Jack's outfit. He's sent out that same crew to molest every outfit on the road."

Jennifer was looking at him calmly. "I hardly know what you're talking about," she said. "Good night, Kern."

She turned to leave him, and Kern stepped forward quickly, grabbing her by the arms. He said tersely, his face close to hers now, "You're a fool, I tell you. You can't do this. If you kill him, you'll kill yourself. Do you hear?"

She looked up at him, the moon falling over his shoulder, full upon her face. She didn't say anything. She just looked at him, and then he kissed her.

He felt her body stiffen in his arms, as he held her tightly, and then relax. For one moment he thought that she was going to respond to him, but that moment passed. She remained passive, waiting for him to lift his face.

He stepped back then, knowing that she was

dead inside, knowing that all her senses and her feelings were dulled by this one terrible urge for revenge. There would be no peace in her life, no love, nothing, until Trace Bovard had paid the price for Jack Steele's death. He thought of her riding in Bovard's carriage, chatting gaily with him, dining with him, listening to his talk, and hating him as if he were the devil incarnate. He felt a wave of pity sweep over him. He wanted to do something for her, but there was nothing that he could do short of walking up to Bovard with a gun, putting it up against his chest, and blowing his insides out.

That would not do, either, because they would never know, then, that Bovard really was the man behind the raids. They had to know that first before Bovard died.

Jennifer Steele said dully, "Do you kiss Daphne Paxton like that, too, Kern?"

Kern stared at her. He said, "I'm sorry."

"Good night," Jennifer murmured. She turned away and went up the steps into the house. There had been no anger in her voice, no resentment that he'd taken advantage of her. It was as if there were no room in her heart for anything but the one burning passion.

Chapter Eleven

In the morning Tobias Paxton sat in Kern's office, looking over the papers the lawyer Dow had drawn up. He nodded, signed the papers, and then smiled at Kern as he stood up. He said, "I trust, Mr. Harlan, this shall be the beginning of a long and prosperous partnership."

They shook hands, and Paxton went out. The affair had taken less than a half hour. Dow had drawn up the papers earlier in the morning after Kern had contacted him.

The little lawyer, as he was about to leave, gathering up papers in his brief case, said briskly, "So now you have a partner, Kern."

"That's right," Kern said.

"A full partner," Dow murmured, "entitled to his share of the profits, although you apparently will be doing all the work."

Kern shrugged. "I won't be doing any more than before," he observed. "I needed Paxton's money in this business."

"Money," Jason Dow stated solemnly, "is the root of all evil."

Burton Reeves put his head through the doorway and said, "A Captain Randolph Manning out here, Harlan. From Fort McLane."

Kern headed swiftly for the door.

The likable officer from McLane was standing just outside, smiling. He gripped Kern's hand, and he said, "You don't seem to want to come back to McLane, Kern. I thought I'd come here."

"Good to see you," Kern grinned. "Come inside." He pushed a box of his best cigars in front of the Captain and said, "Now what brings you to Nebraska City?"

Captain Manning's face clouded a little. "The Colonel sent me here to check up on that consignment. What's the good news now, Kern?"

Kern shook his head. "No word from the *Robert Grimes*," he admitted. "The last we heard they'd had to pull up for repairs below St. Louis. We don't know exactly how much has to be done, but the repairs must be extensive. We've had no word yet that they've even reached St. Louis."

"Our quartermaster tells me we've got to have those supplies," Captain Manning scowled, "if the Army has to go down to St. Louis and carry the stuff to McLane on their backs. We're that bad off. If we have an early snow and the wagons are unable to roll, we'll be in for a very hard winter at the post."

"We'll be rolling the day after the *Robert Grimes* docks here," Kern assured him. "My wagons are waiting."

"Another thing," Captain Manning told him. "Ajax agents are still hanging around the post trying to get Colonel Howlett to rescind the agreement made with you, and give them the hauling order. They've offered lower rates, but they're afraid to promise that they'll equal your time of fifteen days. That's still your ace card with the Colonel."

Kern looked at him steadily. He said, "In other words, if Rocky Mountain can't make that time of fifteen days, the Colonel is very likely to turn the future hauling contracts over to Ajax Overland."

"That's how it looks to me," Captain Manning said. "I believe the Colonel favors you, but if you can't hold up to the promise you made him he feels that he would be better off to do business with Ajax."

Kern puffed on his cigar. He said quietly, "I think we'll keep our promise, Captain. You can tell the Colonel that."

"Meanwhile we'll do everything possible," Captain Manning stated, "to get that steamboat up here with the cargo. I'm on my way to St. Louis now, and I'll see what I can do at that end."

"You're going east?" Kern asked in surprise.

"Sixty-day leave," Captain Manning grinned. "I've been waiting for it all summer."

Kern nodded. He didn't like the idea of losing his best contact at Fort McLane, but there was nothing he could do about it. With Captain Manning gone and the Ajax representatives on the spot, making all manner of promises to the commanding officer of McLane, there was a good possibility that in sixty days, if anything went wrong with this first shipment, the Fort McLane hauling contract would go to Ajax. That would mean the beginning of the end for Rocky Mountain Freighting.

"When I get back," Manning was saying, "we'll see if we can do a little duck shooting."

"Always promises," Kern smiled, "but it's a date."

The next morning he saw Captain Manning off on the packet *Judy Karl*. He noticed that there were only two boats left at the Nebraska City wharves, the other boats being anxious to get downriver before the winter season set in.

On the wharf, too, he saw Ajax wagons loading up, a long string of them, about thirty-five in number. He noticed, too, that they were picking up a cargo that had been guarded the night before by a watchman for Larrimore Freighting Company. The Larrimore commissary, Ed Danley, was standing by, and Kern said to him:

"Larrimore out of business, Ed?"

Danley shook his head dismally. "We were supposed to have this haul," he explained, "but the shippers are afraid to take a chance with us. Ajax promised to furnish a big escort with their wagons, so the shipper went over to them. We lost the haul."

"Nice business," Kern muttered.

"For Ajax Overland," Danley scowled, "but

not for anybody else. We lose a few more contracts like this and we go out of business. I'll find myself working for Ajax, too, the same as everybody else."

"You can always find a job with Rocky Mountain," Kern assured him.

Ed Danley nodded gratefully. "Don't you go under, Kern," he warned, "or this town is through."

"We don't aim to go under," Kern told him.

Back at the Rocky Mountain yard he saw Tobias Paxton standing near the bull corral watching a Rocky Mountain yardman break in a pair of new bulls. Paxton was dressed in English tweed and his shoes were covered with dust from the yard. Seeing Kern coming up, he waved a cheery hand.

"Looking over the establishment," he smiled. "Anything I can do, Harlan?"

"Make yourself at home," Kern told him. "Stop in the office whenever you want to. Reeves will give you a monthly statement on the business we do so you'll know where we stand financially."

"Good," Paxton nodded. "I'll keep out of your way, Harlan."

Kern went on to the office, thinking that perhaps he'd been wrong even hesitating about taking Tobias Paxton into the company. The Easterner intended to keep out of the way; he would not interfere with the business of the company.

As Tobias Paxton's partner, he would have much more contact with Daphne, which was not undesirable, either. Then when he started to think of Jennifer Steele, he became confused. He wasn't sure why he'd kissed her the other evening. It had been an impulse, and he'd apologized for it. The entire affair should have been forgotten then, but it was not. He found himself thinking of Jennifer much more than he should have, even thinking of her when he was with Daphne on occasions.

He'd seen her with Trace Bovard the day after he'd had his talk with her. She'd ridden past in Bovard's carriage, and she'd been laughing gaily. He felt a chill as he watched them go by.

She had the infinite patience of a tigress stalking her prey. She was making contact with Bovard's friends. She was listening, perhaps asking a question or two now and then when Bovard was not present. She was biding her time.

Two weeks passed after Captain Manning's departure before Kern heard from him. A fast packet had come upriver with the mail from St. Louis, and there was a letter from the officer. It stated that the *Robert Grimes* had managed to get into St. Louis, where repairs were being made, and that she would reach Nebraska City in another week or so.

It was now mid-October, with the weather

getting colder every day. Each morning there was a heavy frost in the Rocky Mountain yard, and Kern thought he smelled snow in the air.

Constantly he was receiving dispatches from Fort McLane asking if there were any news on the food cargo. The post quartermaster came down for a brief stay, but returned after he had received Captain Manning's report from St. Louis.

Kern continued to send his wagons out on the trail, always furnishing escorts with them. He had no trouble with the trail pirates, and he understood the reason why. When they attacked they had to be successful. If they were driven off, or some of them captured and brought in to Nebraska City, and it could be proved that Bovard was behind the raids, he was finished.

Twice in three weeks, however, smaller outfits, taking a chance because Rocky Mountain wagons were getting through, went out on the trail, and were hit and destroyed.

After that only Ajax Overland and Rocky Mountain wagons went out. With the cold weather coming on, too, the shippers held up their orders until the following spring. No more boats came up to Nebraska City. The *Robert Grimes* was still in St. Louis, and the letters from Fort McLane were becoming more urgent.

The mail boat came in on a Saturday noon with the report that the *Robert Grimes* was steaming upriver, and would reach Nebraska City on Monday at the latest.

Monday came and passed, with Kern's wagons lined up in the yard, ready to roll down to the wharf to pick up the freight as it came off the boat. On Tuesday evening a trail driver rode in with the news that the *Robert Grimes* had stuck on a sand bar below Hat Island.

Everett Green tossed his hat into the air in disgust when they received the news. He said to Kern grimly, "That's a devil boat, Kern. She'll never get here until the snow flies and it's too late to move."

"We have to roll that freight out to McLane," Kern scowled, "if we have to shovel our way through ten feet of snow."

"It might come to that, too," Green said tersely. "All the signs point to an early winter, and a tough one. For the last thirty years Little Elk's band of Cheyennes have winter-camped up on Bull Creek. They've gone farther south this year. They know."

"Buffalo left early this year, too," Tom Moran pointed out, "and their hides are thicker. That always means plenty o' snow."

Tobias Paxton had not been in the office for more than a week. He came in now, and he shook his head dubiously when he heard the news. He said to Kern, "Think we can get wagons up to Fort McLane this winter yet? We'll be using fifty wagons and a couple of hundred head of stock. That would be a tremendous loss if you were caught in the snow."

"We can't look at it that way," Kern told him. "The Army needs this food. They're depending upon us to deliver it, and I made a promise."

Paxton frowned a little. "No fault of ours the *Robert Grimes* was held up for over a month," he pointed out.

"No one's fault at all," Kern said. "Just a run of hard luck all along. We'll hope the *Robert Grimes* is able to get here before the first snow starts to fly."

"You wouldn't roll if there was snow on the ground, would you?" Paxton asked him.

"We'll roll," Kern assured him. "This early in the winter there might be a thaw. It's hard to tell."

"A thaw," Everett Green growled, "or another big one on top of the first." He added dryly, "That's how our luck has been running this fall."

Kern didn't say any more on the subject, but he noticed that Tobias Paxton was not too well pleased.

When the partner went out Green said thoughtfully, "Thought he was supposed to let you run the business."

"He has," Kern stated. "This is the first time he's ever made any comments."

"First real big shipment we've had," Green

pointed out. "Those other hauls were only child's play compared to this."

"He's worried," Kern explained, "and I don't blame him. If we lose fifty wagons and all that stock, we'll go under. He knows that much about the business."

"Never took him for a fool," Green murmured. "Maybe you did, Kern."

Kern went out to look at the wagons. He'd had his best stock overhauled for this job. Many of the wagons had been newly painted, with new wheels, axles, and tongues installed at considerable expense. They were lined up along the rear fence of the yard—two rows of them, empty, standing close together to conserve space in the yard, ready to roll. Some of them were new wagons, never having been used as yet, that had come off a river steamer three weeks back, Kern having ordered them in St. Louis after receiving Paxton's money.

Green, standing beside him, said, "The stock is well rested, and the men are rarin' to go, too. With any kind of break in the weather you should make that time of fifteen days out to McLane."

"We'll make it," Kern said.

That night there was a light flurry of snow and a high wind. Kern sat in the hotel dining room with Daphne Paxton, looking out the window, scowling at the snow. It didn't last long, but the wind blew fitfully.

Daphne said, "You're worrying too much, Kern. You can't do anything about the weather."

"I hate to sit quiet," Kern growled, "when there's so much to do. I should be out on the trail with my wagons, heading for McLane now."

Sitting here with Daphne Paxton, he found he was bored. He was growing tired of the town and of people, of the monotony of the office, and he wanted to be away. He wanted to buck this weather and the hard conditions of the early winter trail.

Then he noticed that Daphne Paxton was pouting across the table from him, displeased because he was thinking of his business and not of her. Had Jennifer Steele been across the table from him now, they would have been discussing this big haul, the problems they would meet en route. Both would have been interested in it.

Daphne said softly, "You haven't noticed my new dress tonight, Kern."

He left early, and he had a cup of coffee in the big kitchen with Amos Scott before going to bed. He went outside on the porch for a few moments, too. The snow had stopped, and the sky was clear, but a high wind was coming off the river, tearing around the corner of the house. He could see the river from the porch, the water black, ruffled by the wind. It was empty. It was clear enough now for a steamboat to navigate at night, and there was the possibility that the *Robert*

Grimes's captain, anxious to reach his destination and get back to St. Louis, would keep his boat moving if he'd been able to get it off the sand bank.

Kern went to bed. He was awakened hours later by the ringing of a bell in the distance. He could hear the bell against the hammer of the wind against the house.

Sitting up in bed, he listened carefully, definitely identifying it as the fire bell. Then he crossed to the window, lifted it, and listened. He could hear the voice from the main street:

"Fire! Fire! Fire in the Rocky Mountain yard!"

Bolting out of bed, Kern climbed into his clothes, his face gray. He went down the stairs three at a time and sprinted through the door. Coming out on the main street, he noticed that the fire equipment was already being rolled out by sleepy-eyed volunteer firemen. The crowd was rushing down toward the river and the Rocky Mountain yard. Kern could see the red glare in the sky above his yard. The glare was coming from the corner where he'd lined up his fifty wagons for the McLane haul.

Everett Green, tearing out of the boardinghouse at which he lived, fell in step with Kern as they raced for the yard. Green gasped, "Wagons don't burn by themselves, Kern."

Kern had been thinking that same thought. This fire had undoubtedly been started. When they reached the yard they saw a dozen or so Rocky Mountain yardmen running up with buckets of water. A half dozen of the big Murphy wagons at one end of the line were blazing furiously, and those few buckets of water were futile.

Kern roared, "Get those wagons out of the line! Roll them away!"

He grabbed at dazed men who were running in different directions, sending them spinning toward the wagons in question. A half-dozen men raced up, grabbed the wagon tongue of the last burning wagon in the line, and then heaved forward, dragging it out of the line and over toward the empty bull corral.

Kern himself joined another group that had run for a second wagon that had just caught fire. There were four men in this group, and they couldn't get the wheels rolling. Bull Shannon rushed up, knocked two of the men aside, and grasped the tongue. The wheels started to move, gathered momentum, and came out of the line, rolling down a small incline to smash into the first wagon that had been pulled out.

Everett Green yelled at Kern, "Damned lucky the wind's blowing the other way."

Kern noticed for the first time that the wind had suddenly changed direction, and instead of driving south across the line of wagons, it had veered away, thus protecting the remaining wagons from flying sparks.

Tom Moran, Shannon, and Green, along with twenty or thirty Rocky Mountain yardmen and willing spectators, dragged the burning wagons away from the rows. Several other wagons had caught a few sparks, but these were quickly doused with buckets of water. The big crowd that had gathered stood back now, watching the six big wagons burning to the ground.

Everett Green came over to Kern and said grimly, "What do you think, Kern?"

"That fire was started at the north end of the second row of wagons," Kern stated slowly, "and the wind had been blowing from that direction. The one who set fire to the wagons expected that strong wind to throw sparks over every wagon in the line, destroying all of them."

"When the wind changed direction," Green nodded, "we were saved, but it could have been very bad."

They watched one wagon suddenly collapse, sending a shower of sparks out across the fence and into the river. Then another wagon went down, a heap of burning ruins.

"How many men here tonight?" Kern asked suddenly.

"Only the regular watchman," Green told him. "Old Ben McClure. He doesn't see too well to begin with, and it's a big yard."

"Ben's a pretty heavy drinker, isn't he?" Kern asked.

"When he can get it," Green nodded, "which is not too often. Most of the bartenders in this town won't give him credit any more."

"Bring him in the office," Kern said. "I want to talk to him."

Tom Moran came up, and Kern said to him, "Was this yard gate locked tonight?"

"Locked every night," Moran told him. "Closed it myself last night."

"What about the office door?" Kern wanted to know.

"Reeves locks that," Moran said. "But it wouldn't be so damned hard gettin' in here, Kern, if anybody wanted to climb the fence. Nobody goin' to see 'em, especially with Ben McClure drunk in the wagon shed."

Kern glanced at Everett Green. "So Ben was drunk," he murmured. "See if you can sober him up a little, and then bring him in the office."

"Only thing will sober Ben up," Moran grinned, "is more drink. I'll have to get him a bottle."

"Who has the keys for the yard gate and for the office?" Kern asked as Moran was about to go away.

Tom Moran thought for a moment. "Nobody," he said, "but you an' Reeves."

Kern nodded. "All right," he said. He watched Green lighting up a cigar, the red glare of the burning wagons making his lean face ruddy.

"Never liked the looks of that Reeves," Green

observed. "Now, who would want to burn out Rocky Mountain Freighting, aside from Ajax Overland?" He paused, and he said significantly, "There's Bovard now."

Kern spotted Trace Bovard at the edge of the crowd, talking with a few other men. He hadn't spoken to Bovard since the fight outside the saloon, and Bovard had not come near him.

As they were pushing their way through the crowd, Bovard called, "Hard luck, Harlan."

Kern slowed down and looked at him steadily. He saw the cold, sardonic humor in Bovard's eyes, and then he took a long stab in the dark. He said, "Hard luck, but we know the man who set those wagons on fire."

"Do you?" Bovard murmured. His face showed nothing as he smoked on his cigar.

"Now," Kern smiled coldly, "we have to find out who paid him to do it."

"That should be interesting," Bovard observed. "I wish you luck."

Kern passed on, and Everett Green said over his shoulder, "Didn't know we knew who started that fire, Kern."

"We don't know," Kern told him.

Green looked mystified.

Kern said coldly, "The man who set those wagons on fire will be dead in the morning, Everett."

Everett Green scratched his jaw soberly as

they went into the office. He said thoughtfully, "Reckon that's so, Kern."

Tom Moran and Bull Shannon came in a few minutes later with old Ben McClure. The old man was shaky, confused, still half drunk. He was shriveled up, in his late seventies, a tuft of gray hair sticking up out of his bald head.

"Ain't done nothin' wrong, Mr. Harlan," he mumbled plaintively.

The door opened behind them and Tobias Paxton came in. He looked sleepy-eyed, and his hat was askew. The usual cravat was missing from his shirt. He said confusedly, "Terrible. Terrible, Mr. Harlan. What was our total loss?"

"Six wagons," Kern told him briefly. "We could have lost the whole string."

"How did it start?" Paxton wanted to know. "We'll have the law on them."

"We're trying to find that out," Kern scowled. He said to Ben McClure, "See anybody in the yard tonight, Ben, after closing?"

"Nobody," the old man muttered. "Nobody at all, Mr. Harlan."

"He's been sleepin' half the night in the shed," Moran growled. "He didn't even know there was a fire until we woke him up just now."

"Had an empty bottle beside him," Bull Shannon put in.

"Thing is," Tom Moran murmured, "how in hell was he able to get a bottle o' liquor when payday ain't till tomorrow? Didn't know Ben had any credit in this town."

"He don't," Shannon growled. "Not that I know of."

"Where'd you get the money for that bottle?" Kern asked the old man.

McClure looked vacant for a moment, and then his faded, whiskey eyes fell on Tobias Paxton. Paxton stepped forward a little before McClure could speak. He said apologetically, "I'm afraid I'm the culprit, Harlan. I gave Ben a dollar last night before closing. Of course, I didn't know he'd be drunk on duty."

Kern frowned. He said, "All right, Ben. Sleep it off now."

The old man stumbled out of the room.

Tobias Paxton said worriedly, "If I'd known he was going to buy liquor with the money I never would have given it to him."

"Can't do anything about it now," Kern told him. He said to Moran, "I want three sober men in this yard every night from now on—armed men."

"I'll line 'em up," Moran nodded. He went out with Shannon.

Everett Green said casually, "We still know who did it, don't we, Kern?"

Kern looked at him. "We know," he said.

Paxton moistened his lips. He said quickly, "If you know who started the fire, why don't you turn him over to the authorities?"

"We have to know a little more first, Mr. Paxton," Green smiled coldly.

"Who—?" Paxton started to say, and then he stopped.

Very clearly the three men in the room heard the short, quick blasts of a steamboat whistle from a point downriver.

Everett Green yelled, "The *Robert Grimes!*"

He raced for the window and lifted it. Kern joined him there and they stared out across the yard down toward the river. Three more quick blasts came from around the bend, and then the white steamboat came into view, its fire doors glowing red against the darkness of the river casting a reddish glow over the water.

It was a big boat, with three decks and two stacks, looming even larger in the darkness. Already she was sounding her landing bells, and the crowd from the Rocky Mountain yard was thronging down toward the wharf. A shower of sparks gushed up from the *Robert Grimes*'s twin stacks. There were more bells.

Kern Harlan said quietly, "Mr. Green, roll your wagons down to that boat and start loading."

"Right," Everett Green grinned, and then the grin faded.

Both men had been leaning out the window, watching the big packet come in. They both felt it at the same time, and both looked up at the darkening sky. Something soft and cold and wet had touched Kern's cheek, and then he felt it again.

Green said slowly, "Snow."

Behind him Kern heard Tobias Paxton's voice. Paxton was saying, "Too bad. That's too bad."

It wasn't what he said, but it was the way he said it; Kern could have sworn he detected a note of triumph in his voice!

Chapter Twelve

Fifty men worked through the remainder of the night, the snow flying around the flickering torches that had been set up on the wharf. The Rocky Mountain wagons had been drawn up on the wharf, and the roustabouts toiled back and forth across the planks of the *Robert Grimes*, boxes, caskets, barrels on their backs, sweating despite the cold.

Captain William Ambers of the *Robert Grimes* said to Kern in his cabin, "Surely you don't intend to move those wagons in the snow, Mr. Harlan?"

Kern shook his head. "This might stop in the morning," he stated. "We want to be ready to move out with the first signs of clear weather."

"You can't roll through snow," Captain Ambers pointed out. "Those wagons will be heavily loaded, too."

"This might just be a flurry," Kern told him. "If it's only an inch or two deep and the ground freezes up, we'll make good time to Fort McLane."

"If you don't get more snow," Captain Ambers said gravely. "You know this Midwestern country, Mr. Harlan, and the unpredictable weather we're liable to get."

"We'll have to take our chances," Kern said grimly. "They're waiting for this cargo up at McLane. We're going to deliver it."

They went out on the texas deck and stood in the snow, watching the men below. Bull Shannon and Moran and many of the other Rocky Mountain teamsters had joined in to help the roustabouts. About half of the wagons had already been loaded and rolled over to one side, the patient oxen standing dully in the snow.

Everett Green called up jocularly, "We should have reindeer in the traces, Kern."

Kern nodded. He walked over to the railing and put his finger into the little ridge of snow that had formed there. It was about an inch deep, with the snow still falling heavily. The wind had died down and it was getting colder. Despite the fact that it was past six o'clock in the morning, it was still dark.

Captain Ambers, bundled in a heavy coat, was saying gravely, "I'll have my boat moving downriver as soon as this snow stops. I don't want to be caught up here either."

Everett Green came across the planks and up the stairs to the texas deck. He said to Kern, "We should have this load on by nine o'clock. You figure on moving out today?"

Kern looked up into the sky. "We'll see how it is by noon," he said.

"Wouldn't hurt to get a few hours' sleep,"

Green observed. "It'll be a tough trip, Kern."

Kern smiled grimly. "The days of sleeping are over," he said. "We have to roll now."

A man in a heavy bearskin coat was hurrying across the planks, coming up the stairs to the texas. It was only when he was striding across the slippery deck that Kern recognized him as Colonel Tobias Paxton.

Paxton was waving his hand excitedly as he came up, and Green said softly, "Reckon this is trouble, Kern?"

Tobias Paxton said sharply, "Why are you loading these wagons, Mr. Harlan?"

Kern looked at him. "We have an order to haul this cargo up to Fort McLane, Mr. Paxton. You know that."

"In the snow?" Paxton snapped. "This is ridiculous!"

Kern put one hand on the railing and brushed away wet snow. He was looking down at the wagons. He said, "Since when, Mr. Paxton, do you tell me how to roll freight?"

Snow flecked Tobias Paxton's gray beard. It clung to his eyelashes. He said tersely, "Are you forgetting, Mr. Harlan, that I am a partner in this company, and that these wagons and stock are half mine? I do not intend to lose my investment because of a foolhardy undertaking such as this."

Kern felt the anger beginning to rise inside. He

said slowly, "We're not rolling, Mr. Paxton, until the snow stops."

"It might stop and start again in a few days," Paxton told him, "when you're out in open country. We'll lose every head of cattle in the outfit, and those wagons will stand in the snow all winter and fall apart in the spring thaw."

"That's a chance we'll have to take," Kern told him grimly. "This is an Army order. These supplies have to reach Fort McLane. They're on short rations now."

"They'll have to abandon the post if they can't stay there," Paxton scowled. "I absolutely forbid you to take these wagons out of Nebraska City, Mr. Harlan."

"You forbid me?" Kern asked softly.

"As a partner in this enterprise," Colonel Paxton said authoritatively, "I forbid you."

Kern stared at him for a few moments. He heard Everett Green start to whistle softly at his elbow, and then Green said, "Want me to stop loading, Kern?"

Kern looked at him, his jaws clamped. He said tersely, "Load your wagons, Mr. Green." Then he walked toward the staircase and down to the lower deck. He heard Colonel Paxton calling after him furiously:

"Mr. Harlan! Mr. Harlan!"

Striding across the planks toward the shore, Kern saw old Ben McClure hobbling toward him, coming between a break in the line of wagons. The old watchman was waving his arms wildly as he ran, evidently much agitated. He yelled at Kern:

"He's dead, Mr. Harlan, dead as hell out in the bull corral! Just found him there, snow all over him."

"Who?" Kern asked.

"Mr. Reeves," McClure mumbled. "Lyin' there in the snow with a bullet hole in his head."

Everett Green had come across the planks behind Kern. He came up, hearing McClure's words, and he looked at Kern significantly.

"Burton Reeves," he murmured. "I'd say he knew something about that fire, Kern."

Kern nodded slowly. "They wouldn't even wait to make sure that we knew," he said slowly. "Reeves went over to Bovard's side, and he paid the price."

"It was Reeves's key that opened the door," Green observed, "and maybe Reeves who started the fire in the wagons. Somebody had to get old Ben McClure out of the way, though, because if Ben was awake he would have spotted the fire before it really got under way. They didn't want anybody to see that fire until it was really burning."

Kern had started back toward the Rocky Mountain yard. He stopped suddenly, the significance of Green's remark catching up with him. He said slowly, "What are you driving at, Everett?"

Green shrugged. "How did Ben McClure get that liquor?" he asked stubbornly. "How is it Paxton just happens to give Ben money the night there's a fire in the yard?"

Kern scowled. "Doesn't make sense," he muttered.

"Add that," Green told him, "to what Colonel Paxton told you just now. He doesn't want these wagons to go out. You know what happens, don't you, if Rocky Mountain doesn't take this cargo out? Ajax gets the consignment. They have a man out at Fort McLane right now, waiting to hear that you're afraid to roll your wagons in a few inches of snow."

Kern Harlan didn't say anything. He stood there in the snow, listening to the shouts of the roustabouts and his own Rocky Mountain men as they trundled the cargo out to the wagons. He knew what Green was trying to tell him. If he didn't take these wagons out on the trail, Rocky Mountain Freighting was through.

If Colonel Paxton were implicated with Trace Bovard, actually working for Bovard, it meant that Daphne was in on the plot, too. He suddenly remembered Jennifer Steele's early suspicions concerning the girl and the unusual meeting on the trail. He remembered, too, that Daphne had never gone out riding since that incident, which could mean that she was not too fond of horseback riding to begin with, and that that meeting on the trail had been arranged so that she and her uncle could become acquainted with him.

Daphne had been very anxious for her uncle to get into the Rocky Mountain business. She'd been the first one to intimate that he had money to invest.

The whole business was fantastic, and yet there could be a great deal of truth in it. Everett Green was a levelheaded man, and he seemed to believe that Paxton and Bovard were working together.

Kern said slowly, "We'll go back to the office, Everett. I want to look through Reeves's desk. He may have left some papers that will explain what's going on here."

Green nodded. They strode along through the falling snow, past the high Rocky Mountain fence, and then in under the arch to the yard. Kern noticed that it was getting lighter now, and the snow was not so thick. That was a heartening sign.

Green said hopefully, "Might stop altogether in another hour, Kern."

Ben McClure showed them where Burton Reeves's body was. He had fallen just inside the corral gate, and he lay in the snow on his face. They saw the small purplish hole in his temple on the right side. There was not much blood.

"Rifle bullet," Green said. "None of us heard

the shot down at the wharf, but there was a lot of noise down there, and this snow would muffle a rifle shot considerably."

Kern left orders with McClure to have Reeves's body taken into the wagon shed and the undertaker notified. They went into the office then, and Kern lighted a lamp in the outer office. They passed on into Reeves's little cubbyhole of an office, where he kept his books and accounts. A light was burning in here, indicating that Reeves had been in the room before going out into the yard to be shot.

Green said suddenly, "He was walking toward the stables, Kern, when they shot him. I think there was a chance he was trying to get out of town with one of our horses. Bovard would have been watching for him on the wharf where the *Robert Grimes* is tied up. That's the only boat on the river now."

Kern thought about that, and it made sense. Burton Reeves had known what it meant to cross Trace Bovard. Bovard didn't wait for a man to make a confession that implicated him.

"He may have thought he could get down to St. Louis with a pack horse or two and supplies," Kern nodded. "They were watching him every moment."

In Reeves's office they opened his desk, pulling out books, papers, old records, one by one. They found some correspondence between Reeves and a brother he had living back East, but that was all. There was no will, nothing that would in any way implicate him with Ajax.

Outside they could hear the snow blowing around the corners of the building and the distant shouts of the roustabouts on the wharf. Then Kern heard something else—the soft squeak of the outside door. Everett Green heard it, too, and he looked at Kern quickly. The door leading to the outer office was ajar. Green took one step toward it, and Kern grabbed his arm. He held a finger to his mouth for Green to be quiet, and then he said aloud, "Here are some more papers. These might tell us something."

Everett Green looked at him questioningly. Kern had picked up a sheath of old records, telling of hauls made, number of wagons and men used, days on the trail, and other details.

Kern spoke as if he were reading aloud from this record. He said, "To be opened and presented to the proper authorities in case of my sudden death. Signed, Burton Reeves."

Green glanced toward the door. "That's it," he said quickly. "Read it, Kern."

Kern saw the commissary slide a gun out from inside his overcoat, and then step back into the shadows near the coat tree. He nodded and went on:

"This is to state that for the past three months, while working for Rocky Mountain Freighting

Company, I was actively employed by Mr. Trace Bovard, of Ajax Overland Company, it being my duty to undermine Rocky Mountain Freighting in every possible way."

He took a deep breath and glanced over at Green. He thought he saw the door start to move very slightly, and he went on talking.

"I notified Mr. Bovard in August that Mr. Harlan intended to go to Fort McLane in an attempt to get the McLane hauling contract. There was an attempt made on Mr. Harlan's life on his return journey from Fort McLane.

"I am also acquainted with the fact that Mr. Tobias Paxton, now a partner with Mr. Harlan in the Rocky Mountain Company, is an associate of Mr. Bovard, and is as much responsible for my death as Mr. Bovard."

The door opened quickly then, and Colonel Paxton stepped into the room, a blue-barreled Navy Colt in his hand, his bland blue eyes deadly cold now. He was about to open his mouth to say something, and then he noticed that Kern was alone in the room.

Everett Green called from the corner, "Drop that gun, Mr. Paxton, or you'll be deader than Burton Reeves."

He wasn't going to drop it. Kern could see that in his eyes. Paxton was cornered, and ready to fight for his life. From the way he held the Colt gun, he knew how to use it, too.

The Colonel said softly, "A very clever trick, my friends."

His gun was swiveling toward Everett Green when Kern leaped forward, slashing at the gun with his left hand. He managed to knock the barrel down just before it went off, and the slug plowed into the floor. Carried forward by the momentum of his charge, he hit Paxton with his shoulder, slamming him against the doorsill.

Everett Green yelled as Kern grappled with the smaller man, finding him very slippery and considerably stronger than he'd anticipated. Wriggling and twisting, Paxton slipped out of the big bearskin coat, slashed at the oil lamp in the wall bracket, knocking it to the floor, and then broke for the door.

The room was plunged into darkness for a moment, and Kern, falling over the heavy coat, saw the door open and close.

Everett Green called sharply, "He get out, Kern?"

A gun boomed outside just as he spoke. It was the heavy thud of a shotgun, and Kern remembered that old Ben McClure carried a greener with him on his rounds in the yard.

Everett Green said tersely, "That's Ben's gun, Kern."

Throwing open the door, they both raced outside. Ben McClure was running up, the heavy double-barreled shotgun in his hands. Tobias

Paxton lay in the snow about a dozen yards from the office entrance. He did not move.

"Heard that shot inside," McClure growled, "an' I figured this was another one o' them gents who shot up Mr. Reeves."

Kern walked slowly through the snow. Bending down, he rolled Paxton over, looked at him for a moment, and straightened up. He said to McClure, "Reckon that was one of them, all right, Ben. That was Colonel Paxton."

Chapter Thirteen

The snow had stopped at ten o'clock in the morning. At noon, with the sun struggling to break through heavy layers of gray clouds, and three inches of snow on the ground, Kern Harlan sat astride the big bay horse at the head of the column of fifty Rocky Mountain wagons. The wagons were drawn up in a line along the east fence of the yard, stretching from the wharf to a point up past the office.

The spare animals to be taken along on the trip were being driven out of the sheds where they had been put when the snow started. The heavily loaded mess wagon, the cook on the seat, was rolling up to the head of the line.

Everett Green, sitting beside Kern, riding a blue roan, said quietly, "All right, Kern?"

"Ready to go," Kern nodded.

Green looked at him out of the corner of his eyes. "Not worrying about that girl?" he asked.

"It's all right," Kern said briefly.

A half hour before he'd had it out with Daphne Paxton. She'd accosted him in the office, and she'd given him a tongue-lashing over the death of her uncle.

Kern had taken it quietly, calmly, seeing her clearly for the first time. She had a wicked tongue and a furious temper hidden beneath that doll-like exterior. She told him that she wished he and his wagons would rot on the trail.

Green said, "The way I figure it, Kern, Bovard got rid of her, too, when he found that Paxton had blundered and got himself killed. She wasn't of any use to him. I understand she's booked passage on the *Robert Grimes*."

Kern nodded. "She's better out of town," he said.

"She was never Paxton's niece," Green observed. "More likely his wife or his lady friend. They were a pair of sharpers, Kern, and Bovard paid them to work on you."

Kern didn't say anything. He found himself thinking about Jennifer Steele now, wondering if he ought to see her and say good-by. Quite a large part of the town was on hand to watch the wagons roll out. He didn't see her in the crowd.

"Bovard's been keeping himself out of sight, too," Green said. "Nobody's seen him since Paxton was shot."

For one moment after finding Tobias Paxton dead, Kern had thought of going over to the Ajax Overland yard and having it out with Bovard. He'd thought better of it. Reeves was dead, and Paxton was dead, but they still didn't have anything on Trace Bovard. He was in the clear.

There were seventy-five men in the outfit leaving Nebraska City, and it was the largest party Kern had ever taken out on the trail. They were as strong as any of the pirate bands that had been striking at the bull outfits during the late summer and fall, and Kern wasn't too worried about an attack. If it came, he had confidence that they could fight it off.

His big concern was about something else—something soft and white and soundless, falling out of the gray sky, something that you could not fight with guns or with your fists. You could not fight it at all because it did not resist. It just fell and fell endlessly, blotting out the trail, blotting out everything, piling up in huge drifts through which ten teams of oxen could not struggle with a freight wagon.

It was not falling now, and he was thankful for that. The sun had almost succeeded in breaking through the barrier of gray clouds, but this early Western winter was unpredictable. Twelve hours from now the real storm might come—twelve hours, or twelve days from now when they would be unable to turn back or go ahead. That was the nightmare he had to consider.

Years before he'd tried to beat an impending snowstorm with a small outfit of eight wagons. He'd been caught in the blizzard, holed up for six days, and then had managed to struggle through to Nebraska City with his men. They'd found the wagons and the skeletons of the stock the following spring.

At a signal from Kern the big wagons started to roll. Fifty bullwhackers snapped their blacksnake whips. Bull Shannon, handling the lead wagon, roared:

"Fort McLane!"

They rolled through the mud and the snow of the main street, Kern up at the head of the column, Everett Green riding beside him, the wagons strung out in single file behind them, and then the spare stock with the herders moving them along.

As they rode through the crowd lining both sides of the street, Kern looked again for Jennifer Steele, hoping that he would catch a glimpse of her. She was not in the crowd, or she was hidden so well that he could not see her. He was rather silent, almost glum, as he rode from Nebraska City, wondering what was to become of her. She was on his mind the remainder of the afternoon as the outfit rolled slowly toward the Platte.

The snow was uniformly three inches deep on the trail, and it was not too difficult keeping the wagons rolling. Here and there they hit a few soft spots, and it was necessary to add extra teams to push the wagons through.

They made the first night camp at Smith Creek. The creek was not yet frozen over, but the water was slushy with snow and ice.

Kern said to Tom Moran, "We'll use a lot of the spare stock on the wagons tomorrow. Keep shifting them around each day so that all of them get a day's rest here and there."

A half-dozen big fires were started and the cook's mess wagon was rolled into position. Everett Green came up as Kern was sipping a hot cup of coffee from a tin cup. He said, "So far, so good, Kern. I'd say that snow was over for a spell."

Kern nodded. In late afternoon the sky had cleared rapidly, and for a short period the sun came out, shining on the distant snow-covered hills, almost blinding them with the brightness of the reflection.

"We'll make time while we can," Kern stated. "Set a double guard tonight, Everett. Double guards every night on this trip."

"We're seventy-five men," Green half-smiled, "and all tough frontier fighters. You think they'll hit at us, Kern?"

Kern shrugged. "Hard to say, but we're not taking any chances. Keep the stock close to the corral every night. When we get across the Platte we'll move them inside."

The night closed in around them early now. The big fires glowed in the churned-up mud of the enclosure. The night guards rode out into a chilling wind.

Kern walked down to the creek, a cigar in his mouth. He stood there for some moments, looking up into the sky. Dark clouds flew by, blotting out the stars every once in a while. He sniffed the air for the smell of snow, and then he started to make his rounds of the big corral.

When he reached the south side of the circle he heard a horse hammering up the trail, and a moment later the quick challenge of one of his guards. He could hear voices then out in the darkness, and he started to walk toward them, his heart beginning to pound a little. One of those voices sounded familiar.

The rider came on, slowing down in front of Kern. Kern said hopefully, "Jennifer? Jennifer Steele?"

"That's right," Jennifer murmured. She slid from the saddle. In the dusk he could see that she was wearing a heavy woolen coat, Levi's, boots, and a flat-crowned hat. This was the old Jennifer Steele who had ridden in out of the night.

"You made good time," Jennifer stated. "Didn't think you'd reach Smith Creek tonight."

She fell in step beside him, leading the horse as they walked back toward the corral and the burning fires.

Kern said to her, "What brings you out here, Jennifer?"

"I haven't eaten," Jennifer told him. "I could stand a cup of coffee and some chow."

Everett Green stared at her as she came into the circle of light around the nearest fire. The cook set out a tin plate and cup for her, and she spoke as she ate. She spoke calmly, giving them the facts.

"Bovard left town an hour or so before you did, Kern," she said, "and he took with him every available Ajax Overland man. He's to join up with this pirate crew he's had out on the trail. I believe they're camped up in the vicinity of Winfield Creek."

Kern scowled. "He figures on hitting at us, then."

Everett Green said thoughtfully, "With the Ajax men and these frontier cutthroats in his band, he'll have quite a big band. Maybe as high as a hundred and fifty men?"

"Worse than that," Jennifer told him. "From what I've been able to learn, he intends to line up as many as three hundred—roughnecks and breeds—to make this attack on you."

"Three hundred?" Green gasped.

"Where do they intend to hit us?" Kern asked.

"Somewhere on the other side of the Platte," Jennifer said. "It'll take Bovard that long to line up his band. He doesn't intend to let you get through, Kern."

Kern nodded. He sat on an overturned box, looking into the flames. "What else did you learn, Jennifer?" he asked.

"I know he was with the band that attacked Jack's wagon's," Jennifer murmured. "I found that out after he'd left town today. I was quite friendly with one of the clerks in his office."

Kern frowned. "Now you know," he said, "what do you intend to do?"

"Shoot him down like a dog the moment I set eyes on him," Jennifer said promptly. "That's why I came out here."

Kern looked at her. The ice was still in her heart. He watched her sipping the coffee calmly, her hand as steady as his own. He hoped fervently that he would see Trace Bovard before she did.

Everett Green was saying, "So we're safe until we get across the Platte, Jennifer?"

"You're safe," Jennifer told him, "unless you get sixty inches of snow tomorrow or the next day."

Green grinned wryly. "One trouble at a time," he said.

The commissary took a cigar out of his pocket, lighted it, looked at Kern and then at Jennifer, still eating her supper, and then moved away into the shadows with a word to Kern that he wanted to have a look at the stock.

Jennifer sat back after a while, looked over the enclosure, and then said, "Heard you had a little trouble with the Paxtons, Kern."

Kern looked at her. "I was a fool," he admitted. "You were right in the beginning."

"You weren't the first man to be fooled by a pretty face." Jennifer smiled a little. "I saw her getting on the *Robert Grimes* before I left town.

206

What did you do about the partnership with her bogus uncle?"

"I paid her off," Kern scowled. "I borrowed every penny available in town. I'm in debt up to my neck now, but I own Rocky Mountain Freighting. I intend to keep it."

Jennifer nodded soberly. "I think Uncle Billy would like it better that way," she said. She let the coffee cup dangle from her fingers as she sat on the top of a barrel, and she said, "If you lose this outfit now, with your present debts, I suppose you'll go under, Kern."

"I'll go under," Kern nodded, "but I don't intend to lose it."

Jennifer didn't say anything for a few moments, and then she said, "You borrowed money from everybody but me, Kern. I have most of the money you gave me for Steele Freighting last summer. It's yours when you want it."

Kern looked at her. He said slowly, "After the way I acted last summer, Jennifer, I didn't expect that."

Jennifer Steele shrugged. "The money doesn't mean much to me any more, Kern, now that Jack is gone."

Kern rubbed his hands together. "I've lost Uncle Billy, too," he stated. "We're kind of in it together, Jennifer."

Jennifer nodded. They sat there for a few moments in silence, and then she said, "We'd better turn in if you expect to make Beaver Springs tomorrow night."

The sun was shining in the morning, and the sky was blue, flecked with white clouds. Everett Green said as the first wagon started to move, "Looks like the weather is for us, anyway, Kern."

The wind was blowing from the south, and by noon the snow was melting fast, creating another problem. The trail became sticky with mud, and Kern had to put four teams to the wagons instead of three, thus depriving the loose stock of the rest he wanted to give them.

They pushed on steadily, doubling the teams whenever they hit rough spots on the trail, keeping the wagons moving all the time.

Kern sent out an advance guard, and wings on either side to watch for a possible attack on this side of the Platte. At night, on Beaver Creek, he again placed a double guard. He rode with Jennifer most of the day, talking with her occasionally, finding her silences more pleasant than Daphne Paxton's incessant chatter had been.

She knew the trail; she knew how much mileage they had to make before the noonday rest period; she knew the stops, and she knew how much the oxen could endure. At her suggestion, rather than double-teaming at Red Creek, they threw a small corduroy road across the mud coming out of the creek, getting every wagon across safely where there had been the possibility that some might have overturned.

The fourth night they moved into the dead, silent settlement of Fort Hill on the Platte. The traders at the little post had moved back to Nebraska City for the winter, and only a few blanketed Kiowas were there to see them roll in and camp along the river. At night the Platte flowed past the settlement, shallow, muddy, sluggish from the ice farther upriver.

Everett Green said to Kern, "There she is, and we're right on schedule. If we keep up this pace, and we don't run into more snow, we should be in Fort McLane on the fourteenth day, one day ahead of your promise."

Kern looked across the river, wondering what lay on the other side. In the gathering dusk the hills were blotched with patches of snow. It had grown fairly warm again, but this weather was deceptive. Overnight a norther could sweep down on them, choking the trail with snow, upsetting all their calculations.

When Everett Green went back to the wagons, Jennifer Steele joined Kern down at the river. She said quietly, "It might start to get rough from here on, Kern."

"We're ready for it," Kern said. "Let them come."

"They'll outnumber you three or four to one," Jennifer told him.

Kern shrugged. "They're out in the open," he pointed out. "When they hit us we'll be inside a fortress of wagons."

Jennifer was silent for a moment, and then she said thoughtfully, "I have the feeling that it will come pretty quickly after we get across the river. They won't wait until we're close to Fort McLane where we can receive help from the post."

Kern nodded. "Makes sense," he admitted. "We'll be watching for them starting tomorrow morning when we go across."

In the dusk he saw a rider coming across the shallow river, and he recognized the man as Tom Moran. Moran had crossed the river earlier in the afternoon to reconnoiter the other shore.

Kern walked down to the water to wait for him, and he had the feeling as he watched that Moran had news for him.

The teamster came up on the bank, horse snorting. He said briefly, "Trouble brewin', Kern. There's a camp three miles to the north—a big camp. Ain't Injuns, so it must be them damned trail raiders."

Kern broke in half a stick he'd been carrying in his hands. He tossed the two pieces into the water, and he said quietly, "That means they'll hit us tomorrow."

Jennifer put in slowly, "When we're across the Platte, or while we're crossing it?"

Kern looked at her, catching the significance of

her words immediately. If Bovard's crew struck them while they were making the crossing of the river, strung out and unable to maneuver in the shallow water, it would go very hard with them. Very possibly Bovard had this in mind, too.

Tom Moran looked past them at the wagons drawn up in a huge circle just outside the little group of buildings that made up Fort Hill. He said, "Reckon we'd better git across tonight, Kern."

Kern nodded. "Tell the boys to yoke up," he said. "We're rolling." When Moran trotted away he said to Jennifer, "That was smart."

"We're dealing with a snake," Jennifer told him tersely. "Mr. Bovard doesn't make many mistakes. I know him."

Kern smiled at her, glad that she was on his side now—glad for more reasons than one.

Chapter Fourteen

During the early part of the evening Kern sent his wagons into the river, an advance detail having crossed first to protect them in case Bovard's crew should decide to make a night attack.

He rode across with Jennifer and Everett Green, and they sat astride their horses on the north bank, watching the big wagons roll out of the water, the oxen straining as they came up the embankment. The crossing was made as quietly as possible, and by eleven o'clock in the evening the last wagon had come out of the water. They were all drawn up in a circle on a ridge about two hundred yards from the water's edge.

Kern had the stock driven inside the enclosure and a double guard set. Every man in the train slept with his rifle at his side. They awoke to a cold, gray dawn. The sunshine of the previous day had gone. The wind was blowing from the north again, and Kern thought he smelled snow in the air.

Everett Green said grimly, "Trouble always comes in pairs, Kern. You figure on rolling this morning?"

"Can't stay here," Kern told him. "We'll move on until they try to stop us. The longer we stay here, the more chance we'll have of running into a real snowstorm."

The cook fires burned cheerily as the men yoked the teams of oxen and hitched up. When the wagons broke the corral and started to move, Kern rode out with the advance detail. He had two riders out on each wing of the column, riding along the ridges, and a rear guard of four men, watching for an attack from that direction. They rolled steadily toward the northwest as the gray clouds thickened and a few flakes of snow drifted out of the sky.

Tom Moran, with the advance scout, said grimly, "Reckon we're in for it, Kern. This might be the real thing."

Kern was watching a high ridge dead ahead of them. He said, "Where was that camp you saw last night, Tom?"

"About two miles to the east of here," Moran told him. "They know we're comin'. Freight outfits don't travel without noise."

Kern slowed down. He didn't like the looks of that ridge ahead. The trail lifted up across the shoulder of the ridge, and then dipped quite sharply. Behind that ridge a small army could hide. He glanced back toward the line of wagons more than half a mile behind them.

Moran said, "Trouble, Kern?"

Kern shrugged. "That ridge would be a good spot for them to wait," he murmured.

The snow was coming down heavier now—not a real snowstorm as yet, but the white flakes were beginning to fly, tickling their faces as they pointed north.

Moran said thoughtfully, "If it snows hard, Kern, reckon that's all the better for them. They can come out of the storm like the hammers o' hell."

Kern was still staring at the ridge, and he fancied for a moment that he saw a slight movement up there, possibly the movement of a watching head. They were about two hundred yards from the ridge.

"All right," Kern said slowly. "Hold up." He lifted a hand as a signal to the men behind him.

Moran said tersely, "Reckon I'll swing around to the east, Kern, an' have a look at what's behind that ridge."

"Be careful," Kern told him. "Be ready to ride back at the first movement up there."

The snow came at them then in a wave, almost obscuring the summit of the ridge, but just before it came Kern very clearly saw a rider spur over the crest of it, and then another.

Lifting his gun from the holster, he fired three times into the air. Tom Moran, who was less than a dozen yards away, jerked his horse around and started to sprint for the wagons. Kern and the other advance scouts went with him, and as they rode down the grade, Kern could see the wagons already swinging into a circle, the bullwhackers crackling their whips furiously, their hoarse yells drifting up toward him.

Behind, he could hear the whoops and yells of the oncoming raider crew. Bullets started to whistle past them. Turning in the saddle, he sent two shots back at them, and had the satisfaction of seeing one rider slip from his horse.

They came out of the flying snowflakes, ghostly figures, a long line of them, riding hard, intent on reaching the wagons before they could swing into the protective circle.

Everett Green, and Bull Shannon were directing the wagons down on the slope, and they were moving smoothly, flawlessly, a well-drilled team of men, knowing exactly what they had to do and how much time they had to do it.

As Kern reached the nearest wagons they were already drawn into a circle, and the oxen were being unhitched. Teamsters hastily hooked together the rear wheels of the wagon ahead of them with the front wheels of their own wagons. Wagon tongues were facing in toward the center.

Rifle fire already came from the enclosure as Kern and the advance guard hammered in, and the logging chain was drawn across the opening. Bawling cattle milled around in the center of the enclosure. An occasional nervous horse, tied to a wagon, snorted and tugged at its restraining leash.

The Rocky Mountain men dropped down

behind the wagons, and some of them hastily scrambled up to the tops of the loads to fire from that position. The attacking crew came out of the snow, their guns winking orange and red against the dimming light.

Everett Green yelled at Kern, "This is it!"

"Where's Jennifer?" Kern shouted to him.

Green grinned and pointed upward. Kern saw Jennifer Steele's small boot protruding from the top of a loaded wagon, and then he heard her rifle crack. One of the advance riders dropped from his saddle.

The wave broke and swept around both sides of the wagon corral. Bullets smashed into the heavy sides of the wagons, ripped through between wagon-wheel spokes, and two Rocky Mountain men were hit.

Kern caught a glimpse of Trace Bovard riding by, his blocky figure taut in the saddle, riding a big black gelding. Tom Moran, nearby, saw him at the same time, and fired hastily. Bovard kept going, disappearing down the line of wagons.

About a dozen of the crew had been knocked from their saddles. Most of them lay still where they had fallen, the snow whitening their dark figures. One man crawled away on hands and knees.

Then almost as soon as it had begun, the attack died away. They could hear the hammering hoofbeats in the falling snow, and then this, too, ceased. Everett Green looked a little bewildered.

"They have enough?" he asked Kern incredulously.

Kern smiled grimly. "Reckon they'll think it over a little now," he observed. "They were hoping they could catch us before we corraled. Now they'll have to think up something else."

Jennifer Steele scrambled down from the top of the wagon nearby. She came over, ejecting a shell from her rifle, her face smudged with gunpowder. She said calmly, "I missed Bovard as he went by. You see him?"

"I saw him," Kern said. It came to him suddenly that Bovard had made no attempt to conceal himself in this attack, and it meant that the Ajax man had to wipe out this crew so that no one could go back to Nebraska City with the report that he'd been seen with the marauders. He'd committed himself.

"They'll come back again," Jennifer said. "How many men did we lose?"

"Three hit," Tom Moran said, coming up. "Only one of 'em real bad. The other two kin still shoot."

It was snowing hard now, and they could not see more than fifty yards from the enclosure.

Everett Green said morosely, "Might be a big one, or it might be another false alarm."

"Gonna be hard to see 'em when they come in

again," Moran observed, "an' they're still plenty strong."

Kern walked to the chain gate and stared into the blinding sheets of snow. Even if they beat off Bovard's raiders now, they still had the snow to contend with. If it was a big storm, and it closed the trail for the winter, they were finished anyway.

Jennifer came over to him and said quietly, "This is tough, Kern. I guess none of us looked for the snow and Bovard at the same time."

"We'll take them one at a time," Kern murmured. "First it's Bovard."

"He might make a second charge in a matter of minutes," Jennifer said. "He won't like it too much sitting out in that snow either. The sooner he runs over us, the sooner he gets back to Nebraska City."

"Where he becomes head man in the freighting business," Kern Harlan scowled, "and no competition."

He made the rounds of the corral, taking note of the positions the men had taken when the fight started. About a quarter of them had gone up on top of the wagons and stretched out on the tarpaulins over the load to fire at the raiders. The others were down below the wagons, firing between the rails, dragging boxes and barrels from the wagons to form barricades. They were crouched beneath the wagons now, peering over the tops of their slight fortifications, waiting for the raiders.

Kern said to Jennifer, who was walking at his side, "How did you like it up on top of the wagon?"

"Better than down below," Jennifer said promptly. "I could shoot down at them as they came in, and I was a hard target up on top."

Kern nodded, and a small smile came to his face. He said, "We'll have a little talk with Green and Moran and the others."

They went back to the group at the chain gate, and Kern said to Moran, "Lower these chains so that a horse can jump them without any trouble."

Tom Moran stared at him. "We put 'em there," he muttered, "so that this bunch can't jump over."

"Lower them," Kern told him. "We want them to jump over now."

Everett Green said slowly, "You want them to break through, Kern?"

"That's right," Kern smiled. "I want every one of them inside the enclosure."

Green rubbed his chin. "You're the boss, Kern," he murmured. "Tell us about it."

"We have three wagons full of sacked grain for the Army horses. Is that right?" Kern asked.

"Three wagons," Green nodded. "Nine, Ten, and Eleven in line."

"Take about fifty sacks out of the wagons,"

Kern ordered. "Prop them up under the wagons and put hats on their heads."

Tom Moran and Bull Shannon were staring at Kern as if he were out of his mind, but Everett Green and Jennifer Steele were beginning to smile a little.

"What else, Kern?" Green asked.

"I want every man in this outfit up on top of the wagons," Kern told him. "Keep down flat and conceal yourselves when they come in. Count off the men, Green. Every sixth man will fire at the raiders as they come in. The rest will hold their fire and wait."

"For what?" Moran asked bluntly.

"When they find that they can get inside the enclosure through this low chain gate," Kern told him, "they'll probably all come through."

"Then," Green smiled, "we'll give 'em hell from the tops of the wagons—everybody. That right, Kern?"

"That's right," Kern nodded. "It'll be close range inside the corral. Have your rifles and pistols up on the load with you. Fire when I give the signal, but everybody keep down flat so they'll have a hard time seeing you. This snow will cover you up pretty thoroughly in about five minutes if you lie still."

"Sounds good," Green nodded. "If it works, this fight will be over in about ten minutes after Bovard's raiders come in."

"It has to work," Kern told him quietly.

Green, Moran, and Shannon went off to pass on the instructions to the men. Kern watched them as they broke open two of the wagons and hauled out the sacks of grain. One by one the sacks were shoved in under the wagons and propped up against the wheels in a reclining position. Hats were placed on top of the sacks, and from a distance with the snow swirling around the wagons they could very easily be mistaken for riflemen.

At Green's instructions the men started to climb to the tops of the wagons. They flattened out on the loads and lay still, and in a very short time the wet, clinging snow covered them and the tarpaulins.

Kern said to Jennifer, "All right. This is our wagon."

He helped her up to the top and climbed up beside her. Both of them had rifles, and Kern took out his Colt gun, placing it just inside his coat where it would keep dry and at the same time be ready for use at a moment's notice. They lay with their faces toward the center of the enclosure.

As the snow started to whiten them, Kern said quietly, "When they get inside, I want you to do something for me."

"What is it?" Jennifer asked.

"Don't shoot at Trace Bovard," Kern told her. "He's mine."

"No," Jennifer said.

Kern turned his head slightly to look at her. "You'll regret it," he said, "if you kill him."

"Why should I regret it?" Jennifer demanded. "I've thought about this for a long time."

"That's the trouble," Kern said. "That's why you won't forget about it after it's done. We need your rifle up here, but aim at the others."

Jennifer didn't say anything for a long while, and then she said slowly, "He killed Jack, Kern. How can I forget that?"

"You'll have to forget it sometime, Jennifer," Kern observed. "It'll be easier if you don't kill him."

Jennifer Steele was silent for a few moments, and then she said, "I'll think about it, Kern. I'll promise that. Nothing else."

They waited for nearly ten minutes and nothing happened. Lifting his head, Kern looked down along the line of wagons. He could see vague white shapes on the tops of the loads, and if he hadn't known what they were he could not have identified them. He was satisfied.

Jennifer said, "Maybe they won't come. Maybe they'll just sit and wait us out."

"They have to come," Kern told her. "We have enough supplies to last us all winter here. Bovard won't have supplies with him. He has to hit and get back."

They were silent again, and then Jennifer said,

"Funny that I should be thinking of Uncle Billy now."

Kern nodded. He glanced at her, and then he said curiously, "What was the last thing he had to say, Jennifer?"

Jennifer looked at him, took a deep breath, and then looked away. Before she could answer, Kern very clearly heard the hammering hoofbeats. He said briefly, "Here they come."

The raiders opened fire as soon as they came within sight of the wagons. Kern heard the fire returned by about a dozen or so men on top of the wagons. He lay still, looking out over the edge of the load. He could see the logging chain and the opening between the two wagons. Occasionally he saw riders sweeping past about twenty or thirty yards out from the wagons. He saw the flash of the guns against the white of the snow.

Inside the enclosure were over three hundred oxen, closely bunched together, their horns clashing discordantly as they moved around frantically, held in by ropes and poles that had been pounded into the ground.

Between this temporary bull enclosure and the wagons was a space of about fifteen feet, and down this lane the raiders would come when they discovered that they could come over the logging chain gate.

Jennifer said suddenly, "One of them saw it, Kern."

Kern had noticed that, too. One of the raiders, a man in a buffalo coat, riding a spotted horse, had come in close and pointed excitedly to the chains as he went past.

"They'll be coming in soon," Kern murmured.

His own men were keeping up a desultory fire from the tops of the wagons, yelling defiantly, but only about a sixth of his force was in the fight as yet. The others waited, their bodies whitened with snow, concealed up on top of the loads.

The firing died down a bit, and Kern leveled his rifle. He said, "They're drawing off to get instructions. I think they'll make a straight cavalry charge at the opening now. We'll let them all come in if we can."

He saw Everett Green, on the next wagon, lift a hand to him, and he nodded. Down below the frightened oxen were still bellowing, surging against each other, but keeping within the confines of the rope.

Another five minutes passed, and then the hoofbeats came on again, the heavy thudding of riders moving close together. Kern saw them come through the sheets of snow, four abreast, a solid mass of them, heading straight for the chain enclosure. The lead horses leaped the low chain and the others followed, whooping victoriously as they drove in, sweeping around the bellowing oxen in the center of the enclosure, firing at everything that moved.

Lying very still, Kern watched their painted faces flashing by beneath him. They wore white men's clothing, but many of them were Indians or half-breeds, outcasts from their own races, riding now for Bovard's pay.

They swarmed in, a dozen at a time. One of them leaped from the saddle, worked feverishly on the chains, and slipped them from their moorings, enabling the riders following to come in without having to leap over the chains.

A few of the Rocky Mountain men returned their fire from the wagons, but the others still held up, waiting for Kern to give the signal. When he saw Trace Bovard's black gelding coming in through the opening, he started to rise slowly, rifle in hand. The Rocky Mountain men on the wagons saw him clearly as he lifted a hand.

A sheet of orange flame broke out around the inside of the enclosure. Men and horses went down from that first burst, and it was followed immediately by another and another.

Rifles empty, they opened up with short arms, and at close range it became a slaughter. The dazed raiders taking the fire from all sides, clearly exposed in the corral and unable to get clear shots at the riflemen up on the wagons, made a frantic dash for the narrow opening through which they'd come less than a minute before.

Here the havoc was the greatest. About a

hundred and fifty of them tried to bolt through the opening at once, and it was only wide enough to accommodate three or four horses at a time.

The Rocky Mountain teamsters continued to pour that deadly fire into them, emptying saddle after saddle. The raiders dropped to the ground in the midst of churning hoofs, and the mud and the snow around the gate enclosure became mingled with their blood.

Up on his knees, Kern tried to single out Trace Bovard. Occasionally he caught glimpses of the Ajax leader roaring commands at his men, but none of them listened to him now. Panic-stricken, they wanted only to get out of this death trap into which he'd chased them. Kern saw him slash at them with his gun barrel, trying to get them to dismount and take cover underneath the wagons.

Jennifer Steele, at his side, had stopped firing after the raiders broke for the opening in an attempt to escape. She had her rifle in her hand, and as Bovard raced by them, not more than fifteen yards away, Kern saw her lift the rifle. He took a shot at Bovard himself, but his bullet knocked another man from the saddle, and Bovard dashed on unharmed.

The bulls in the enclosure were surging madly against the ropes now, frightened by the incessant shooting and the riders swirling around them. Kern expected it to happen sooner or later, and it happened just as Trace Bovard's big black was shot from underneath him and he was catapulted through the air, his body striking the ground just outside the bull enclosure. It was at that moment that the bulls broke the rope, tearing up the poles that held them.

Kern stood up, his rifle limp in his hand, sick at the sight. The bulls rolled over the spot where Bovard had fallen. Kern heard Jennifer's horrified gasp. The bulls were running in all directions now, unable to break out through the wagons, and with the opening still jammed by the raiders trying to get through.

Kern yelled to Bull Shannon, on the next wagon, to close up the gate when the last of Bovard's crew was through. He saw Shannon nod and clamber down.

After the last raider had disappeared outside, Shannon picked the heavy chains from the mud, slipping them in place again. The Rocky Mountain men sat where they were on the tops of the wagons, waiting for the bulls to quiet down.

Everett Green looked over at Kern, lifted a hand in acknowledgment, and then shook his head as if he, too, were repelled by the carnage.

Kern could hear Jennifer breathing hard at his side. He said to her, "All over now."

She just nodded, and they sat there in the flying snow. Her face was gray, and she was shaking a little. The guns had stopped all around them, and the only sounds they could hear were the bellowing of the oxen.

After a while the cattle quieted down, too.

That night they sat around the big cook fires. The snow had stopped at about five o'clock in the afternoon, leaving a deposit of about three inches.

"Not too bad," Everett Green said. "We can roll in the morning."

Kern nodded. He sat with Jennifer before the big fire long after the others had turned in for the night. He finished up another cup of hot coffee and placed the tin cup on a box in front of him. He looked up into the rapidly clearing sky. The stars were shining through rifts in the clouds, and after a while a sliver of moon came out.

Kern said, "What was it Uncle Billy said to you, Jennifer? You were telling me before the raiders came in."

Jennifer Steele hesitated. She smiled a little, and then poked at the fire with a stick. She said, "It—it was rather personal, Kern."

"I'd like to know," Kern persisted.

She looked at him almost sheepishly, and then she said, "He told me that I should marry that young fool."

Kern stared at her. "What young fool?" he asked.

"You," Jennifer murmured. "Your Uncle Billy knew you were a fool as far as women are concerned."

Kern sat there for a moment, looking at her. He said, "What did you tell him, Jennifer?"

Jennifer Steele frowned and looked away. She murmured, "I told him I would if he wanted me."

Kern Harlan smiled a little. "I've been a fool," he admitted, "but I don't always have to be a fool." He reached over and took her hand. He said, "I've always done what Uncle Billy wanted me to."

"I've had the greatest respect for Uncle Billy's wishes, myself," Jennifer said softly. "I rather liked his choice." She was smiling at him.

He had the feeling that this was the way it always had been with her, and that deep down he'd felt the same way about her. Their quarrels and their disagreements had only been on the surface. This, now, was full and rich and forever. He liked it that way.

Center Point Large Print
600 Brooks Road / PO Box 1
Thorndike, ME 04986-0001 USA

(207) 568-3717

**US & Canada:
1 800 929-9108**
www.centerpointlargeprint.com

czlg

ROLL THE WAGONS

Center Point
Large Print

Also by William Heuman and available from Center Point Large Print:

Heller from Texas
Guns at Broken Bow
On to Sante Fe
Then Came Mulvane
Gunhands from Texas
Bullets for Mulvane

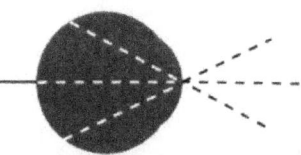

**This Large Print Book carries the
Seal of Approval of N.A.V.H.**